THE EXPANSION BOOK 1
RECON

DEVON C FORD

V
PRESS

VULPINE

PRESS

First published by DHP Publishing in 2018
Published by Vulpine Press in the United Kingdom in 2020

Cover image by Jamie Glover at eruleanfuture.com
Cover by Claire Wood

ISBN: 978-1-83919-332-3

www.vulpine-press.com

"The Earth is the cradle of humanity, but mankind cannot stay in the cradle forever."

Konstantin Tsiolkovsky

PROLOGUE

Lunar Arrivals Port

"What was that?" Jake Santana asked, his ears pricking up and his brow knitted.

"What was what?" Jamie Paterson answered. His head was half-buried in a shipping container full of machine parts.

"I heard it too," the young ensign, Kyle Torres said ominously. "It sounded like it came from the arrivals area. Come on."

The three of them walked out of the freight hangar, where the pilot and crew of the detained ship were waving their arms and shouting about their rights being infringed. Jake and the others ignored them, hearing more sounds that made their spines tingle.

"Something ain't right," Jake said. His left hand dropped to the service pistol holstered on his thigh and hovered there. The standing orders not to draw a weapon unless fired upon echoed around his skull. He didn't draw it, but he kept that hand on the grip, which made him swing the other arm awkwardly as he ran. They rounded a corner, hearing shouts of alarm interspersed with gunfire, then put their heads down and ran the two-hundred-meter length of the tunnel separating them from the main part of the lunar space port.

"Alpha one from alpha one three," Torres squeaked into his radio mic, the panic making his voice sound younger and more vulnerable than he already was.

Jamie looked to him, and received a shake of the head when no answer came. Jamie tried his own radio, shouting the hail louder and more firmly than Torres had done. He repeated the call, but heard nothing back.

As they neared the end of the tunnel, all three breathing heavily from the run, Jake decided to complete the trifecta and try his own radio.

"Alpha one fr—"

A scream tore the air, a person bellowing in guttural pain or anger, followed by the high-pitched, chattering thrum of automatic gunfire.

Their radios erupted as one and the gravelly sound of their commanding officer's voice filled their minds.

"All hands, this is Commander Dassiova. Lunar Port is under attack. I say again, we are under attack. All hands: battle stations. All hands: *battle stations.*"

The warning sobered everyone who heard it. Jake, Torres and Jamie all drew their sidearms and stacked up against the wall at the corner before Jake nodded and stepped out with his gun raised. Another metallic chatter of rapid-fire rounds answered his movement, shattering the tiles of the wall and punching holes through the cover where his head had been only moments before.

"One shooter," he said, gasping for breath among the dust. "Automatic weapon. Thirty meters."

"Draw fire," Torres said, his voice rising in the panic.

"No," Jake snapped. "Keep your head down."

"We need to move, Seaman," Ensign Torres said, a hint of sudden fire in his words.

"The wheel's right," Jamie said as he mocked the young officer. "We're pinned down here, and that rifle will puncture the dome if we don't take him out soon."

Jake thought about it, his mouth set into a thin line as he considered what he had to do. He didn't like it one bit.

"You two break for cover over there," he said as he pointed across the wide tunnel intersection. "I'll take the shot."

They took off, running low and fast and holding their breath for the few seconds it took for the shooter to dial in their location. The gun sounded again, plumes of debris erupting behind the two runners and growing dangerously close to their heels as they darted across the space. Jake took a breath and stepped out. His gun was up, sighting along the barrel held steady in both hands to where the shooter had been. He squeezed off five fast rounds.

The chattering gunfire stopped abruptly as the shooter fell to the ground. Jake took two long breaths, staring at the body of the first person he had killed up close. After a beat, he started toward him.

When he was ten paces away the body blossomed in slow-motion, expanding outward in flame as the explosives strapped to his chest detonated. It was only a small charge, but it was enough to blow the body apart and fling the twisted remains of the automatic rifle past Jake's head. The velocity would have killed him if he had been just a pace to his left. The other two caught up with him. Jamie said nothing, but Ensign Torres looked ashen. Jake steeled himself and took off at a dead run toward the sound of more gunfire and screams.

⁓

Petty Officer Class Two Leslie Brandt waved two of the grunts from their squad forward. They had done this with a dozen inbound ships on their first day on duty. The most effective way to deal with passenger transport was to bring all of the passengers off and search the ship. They would then separate crew and civilians before searching them through a form of immigration, where their travel documentation and identification scans were completed. It was laborious, time-consuming and none of them felt good about detaining the civilians travelling to and from the Moon. After all, they were just going to work after it had been opened up for commercial travel less than half a year ago.

Most of the construction teams rotated every six months. They lived and worked on the surface of the Moon under the domes and new energy shields, but the human traffic between the Moon and Earth was still relatively new and subject to security measures.

Through her earpiece, Brandt heard that another ship was inbound, this one bearing a construction team due to swap with the raucous group currently in departures. Their banter made it clear the waiting group was eager to get back planet-side and spend the double wages they'd earned over the last half-year. There was barely anything on the surface of the Moon to spend them on. One of the other squads was patrolling and searching other areas, and Brandt didn't know if she or they had drawn the short straw. She left a third seaman overlooking the ship being searched as the passengers clutched their luggage and waited in line to be processed.

Brandt walked toward the newly arrived ship as it taxied through the airlock. The door popped its seal, hissing as it opened, and the metal staircase was rolled toward the opening. Brandt prepared to go through the same scripted speech, pulling the card from her leg pocket beneath the holstered sidearm, and putting on her fake smile.

"Welcome to Lunar Arrivals," she began. "On behalf of the combined terr…"

She didn't finish her greeting. Gunfire erupted from the dark recess inside the ship above her, spraying out wildly and causing instant chaos inside the arrivals hangar. Brandt went down, two small rounds puncturing her lower torso, but miraculously missing everything vital. Her head hit the edge of the steps and knocked her out cold as rapid footsteps stomped down the metal ladder.

The group calling themselves The Freedom to Choose was the cause for the heightened terrorist threat their unit had been briefed about. The group had made public declarations of hostility toward the four main colliders on Earth, the energy source creation machines established to create and harness singularities. This threat had resulted in entire divisions of the United Nations Peacekeeping Force being deployed to push the no-go and no-fly zone out miles further away from the enormous machines.

The Freedom to Choose objected to humanity pushing the bounds of their natural state and leaving the planet to colonize the closest body in space. They were mostly just making noise until the plans to create the energy-domed colonies on Mars were announced.

Then the splinter faction of the group, The Choosers, decided on a militant approach. They took up arms to hamper the efforts of the UNPF and private corporations as they spread humanity's metaphorical wings across the galaxy.

What had started as a legitimate political movement, like countless other times in human history, had festered and mutated away from its original goals to become something far more dangerous and corrupt than anyone could have envisioned.

The singularity drives, powered by the new energy source in mass production all over the globe, were capable of continual acceleration in the vacuum of space. This allowed for a journey of less than six hours to reach the Moon. This new technology put Mars colonization well within reach, and the teams working to build the domes to sustain life had been there for almost a decade already, building the basic infrastructure before the expansion plan kicked into high gear.

The Mars program was officially based at the lunar base and was predominantly staffed by private companies with little to no UNPF or CTSF, the Combined Territories Security Forces, interaction. They operated on the Moon because it was the one place left they could work outside the law; they claimed their own land and made their own rules just like in the wild west.

But still, The Choosers had never conducted military-scale attacks before, and Brandt's men and women were unprepared, poorly armed and caught totally by surprise.

Armed men and women sprayed indiscriminate bullets everywhere as they flooded off the transport shuttle and into arrivals.

From the way The Choosers conducted the attack, it was obvious they were on a suicide mission. After the duty unit responded and drew their sidearms to concentrate their fire at the foot of the metal stairs, the invaders' intention was clear. One of the terrorists was hit, collapsing forward with flailing limbs to make the others scatter panicked away from their downed body. Seconds later the attacker detonated, a suicide vest rigged to their biometrics blowing savagely as the heart stopped and the bomb timer started. The terrorists continued the attack, spreading out and overwhelming the too-few defenders rapidly as pockets of leaderless peacekeepers were pinned down by the superior firepower. There were no heavy-weapon platforms, no automated gun systems and no armed drone surveillance programs operating. The place was still treated as a frontier outstation.

The secured doors leading out of the area closed in their attack. Other than the hangar airlocks, the only other way out was the long service tunnel to the freight arrival dock. A large pallet containing what looked like a bomb was unloaded from the newly arrived shuttle hovering six inches from the ground, courtesy of the four repulser jets at each corner propelling it quickly across the open space toward the dome edge. The way the terrorists treated it with almost equal care and fear combined with the wires and makeup of the device screamed bomb to anyone watching.

The sporadic gun battles had faded, becoming an occasional outbreak of firing as both sides ran low on ammunition. Just as the bomb was bumped into the inner dome, a group of three UNPF burst from the access tunnel and sprayed the three terrorists arming the device. If they weren't stopped it would rip open the dome and depressurize them all out into space.

Jake was sweating and out of breath when he reached the main arrivals hangar, more from the adrenaline than the physical exercise. Glancing around the corner, he realized they were on the near side of what looked like an explosive device. It seemed to be being rigged to blow underneath one of the main support beams of the huge dome. He ducked back and filled the others in.

"Bomb," he said, his eyes wide with adrenalized fear. "They're trying to blow the goddamned dome!"

"We can't let that happen," Torres said, stating the obvious with all the manly gusto he could summon.

"Duh," Paterson said, embarrassing the boy. "Not if we like living."

"On three," Jake said as he gripped his service pistol, which felt inadequate for the challenge. "One, two… *three.*"

They stepped out and opened fire, dropping the three people rigging the device as the small 6mm subsonic rounds drilled into their bodies and expanded on impact. Their bodies exploded before the three ambushers reached them. Jake saw the detonator—the flashing lights of the display indicated 'ready' beside a red button with the clear plastic safety shield raised.

Movement to his right caught his eye as another terrorist burst into view; he was a ragged-looking man about Jake's age but his eyes displayed none of the discipline and belief that the seaman possessed. The two men raised their guns at one another. Both pulled their triggers at the same time, and both guns clicked. Jake's gun had run dry and the old machine gun in the hands of the terrorist jammed. Both men's eyes went wide, and both reacted at the same time.

Jake stepped back, dropping the magazine out and grabbing another from his right hip to slap it forward into the gun. He almost made it but having to keep his eyes on the advancing terrorist threw off his aim and the magazine struck the housing and didn't sit snugly. He glanced down to try and make it fit, to will it into the housing so he could draw back the slide and drill the bastard. He'd keep shooting until the gun clicked dry once more. Jake finally managed to get the magazine in and grip the short slide to feed a round into the chamber just as his eyes met his attacker's. He pulled the trigger, snatching it fast and repeatedly to pump bullet after bullet into his chest.

But the other man didn't go down.

Each report of Jake's pistol was answered by the sound of crackling electricity and a metallic thudding noise. Every shot he fired just bounced off the man who was quickly on him, knocking the gun from his grasp. They grappled. Jake maneuvered to allow the forward momentum of his attacker to become his downfall. He took two fast paces backward, grabbing the man's collar below his snarling mouth and throwing his right leg up and over the man's neck as he spun to bring him down. This was what his training had taught him to do through repetition. They landed in a heap, Jake's strong, conditioned arms and legs wrapped around his thinner opponent.

He doubled down on his hold to choke his scrawny neck between his thighs.

The man was trapped, choking slowly and powerless to break free of the robust hold the soldier had on his throat. His right hand fluttered at Jake's groin, weakly trying to grab his balls and use them as the key to open the lock, but Jake snatched hold of his wrist and pulled it tight.

The terrorist's eyes bulged from the added pressure and pain. His focus darted to the sparking cable lying between the blood and viscera beside them. It had been damaged by the explosion of one of his own people. The man's eyes darted back to Jake's again, just as his left hand made a desperate grab for the cable.

Jake made an instant, instinctive judgment call and released his prisoner, unwrapping his legs and rolling away like he had been electrocuted, which was exactly what he feared. Instead of frying him, though, the terrorist grabbed the cable and thrust the exposed live wire into his own mouth. He jerked like a landed fish, and as the electricity stopped his heart, it also stopped and started the one-second fuse to detonate the device on his chest.

Jake rolled in panic, but he couldn't get away fast enough. Just as he got to his feet in a crouch, the bomb went off. The blast had been contained and shaped to explode outward like a wide blade of unstoppable energy, cutting Jake's legs off in a spray of red mist as it atomized everything between his thighs and his ankles.

His right arm was blown away in ragged, spinning chunks by shrapnel thrown in the blast and some of those same fragments embedded themselves in his back and skull.

His eardrums imploded with the concussive force of the detonation, and the world went dark for him in a blinded instant.

~

Leslie Brandt opened her eyes and blinked herself back into consciousness. The pain ravaged her left flank where the bullets had passed through her flesh. She was dazed, confused, and her eyes focused on the distant view of Jake reloading his pistol faster than she had ever seen.

She saw the muzzle flashes, saw the man who wasn't wearing visible armor keep coming at him. It was like this man was wired on stims in order to feel no pain. Instead of going down, he threw himself at her friend. She saw Jake incapacitate him and smiled a little to herself. There was nobody in their squad better at grappling on the mats than he was. But that smile turned to horror, then to fear as she saw him scrambling to escape.

She watched the explosion, watched his almost limbless body flung away at an odd angle. The ravaged and burned torso spun sickeningly to a stop thirty paces from her. She began to crawl to him, willing her arms and legs to move faster. But just as she reached desperately from a dozen paces away to try and touch him, her consciousness fled and left her in the same inky dark.

CHAPTER 1

The Previous Day, Lunar Approach

"Aw, man," Jamie Paterson said as he craned his neck against the restraints to see out of the small window. "Would you look at *that*."

Jake and Leslie tried to look, but only Paterson's above-average height allowed him to see the lunar docks. Leslie looked at Jake and tried to convey her annoyance through the visor of her helmet. The suit's software had mirrored the glass against exposure to sunlight and all he could see was his own helmet's image reflected back at him.

"Home for the next sixteen months," she said. The armor distorted her normally toneless voice into a tinny sound coming out of the speakers. It was barely audible over the noise of the UNPF lunar transport shuttle, but that internal vibration was nothing compared to the noise it made breaking atmosphere before the five-and-a-half-hour journey to the Moon. The tour for their unit, all one hundred and ten of them, was eighteen months. But for Jake, Jamie and Leslie, who had first met when they walked into basic training in Cuba a little over three and a half years ago, it would be less. Their assigned service was due to end before their deployment did.

Signing their lives away, for five years at least, had been a monumental moment in each of their lives before they were inducted, hazed, bullied, trained and molded into the capable men and women of the United Nations Peacekeeping Force of the American Territories.

When they passed through their intensive training course and waited to find out where they would be scattered to, none of them would have guessed that they would have stayed together the whole time. The three were all given the same assignments until their unit was rotated out of UNPF and into CTSF, the Combined Territories Security Forces, for their overseas tour.

Overseas, in this case, referred to through space. Sixteen months patrolling, searching and monitoring the almost forty thousand people living and working on the Moon's surface.

"And I bet the food is every bit as shitty as we've heard," Jake Santana answered drily, his own suit speakers sounding just as tinny but managing to convey his boredom. A young man with simple needs, Santana had left home after high school to make things easier on his mom, who had his younger siblings to feed and look after. For him, as professional and capable as he was, it was all about the food.

"Cut the chatter, shitbirds," Master Petty Officer Kip Carter growled at them, the speakers on his armor turned up to make his voice carry.

He cut over two junior officers and two less senior NCOs to deliver the reprimand, and all four of those men and women kept their heads facing forward or looked down at the deck. The only signs marking them as different were the white flashes or simple stars painted over their right shoulders. They all wore the same regulation armor with their visored helmets on. The commander had ordered the entire unit to keep their armor and helmets secured and pressurized, after a transport ship from the African territory suffered a pressure loss recently. That incident had killed half a unit, along with their senior Non-Comm. The commander didn't want to take any chances, so his men and women split over two ships had to spend the entire journey closed down inside their rigs, which was uncomfortable and claustrophobic, to say the least.

They cut their chatter, each finding their own thoughts or trying to steal a glance out of the few windows, hoping to see the series of rigid geometric domes that provided most of the livable atmosphere on the Moon.

Their ship, the lead of the two containing the unit and their supplies, swung in and settled horizontally to rotate its back end around on a central axis and reverse slowly on its maneuvering thrusters. It docked into one of the twelve wide hangars sprouting out of the large dome, which was the main space port.

The light through the small windows darkened, and was replaced by the dull blinks of the emergency lighting inside the vast space. Both ships could easily have fit inside there, but safety protocols dictated that incoming flights had to be one ship per landing area. Anything to avoid another preventable but massive loss of life. The commander himself was on their ship, which might have sounded daunting to anyone new to the unit but was the far better option. The command chief, the unit's most senior non-commissioned officer, would be travelling in charge of the other ship, and he was not a man to upset.

With a clank and a hiss from outside the hull—sound carrying once more was evidence that they were back in atmosphere—the struts of the ship flexed under the weight of the ungainly and lumpy transport bird as it settled down. The sounds faded as though everything was powering down, and the loudspeaker on the commander's suit barked loudly into life.

"Welcome to Lunar Port. Now get your shit together and prepare to work."

"Look," Jake said as he dumped his kit bag on the bottom bunk of his rack, "all I'm saying is that it's worth it for the money alone, not to mention all the other stuff."

"Hell, yeah," Paterson answered. "Sixteen long, cold, boring months and I'm going back home to get my degree."

The others rolled their eyes. They had heard this before. Paterson had talked about nothing else for the entire time they had known him, to the point where they probably knew his career and life goals better than the man himself. He'd finished high school, graduating in the top twelve percent in the territory for grade scores, but since he was from a poor family with no political or military connections, he had no chance of paying for his higher education.

He wasn't genius enough to get a scholarship—those had been handed out to ten-year-olds occupying the top one percent—so he did the only thing he could to realize his dream: he joined the UNPF to get sponsorship for his education. He was clever, annoyingly clever in fact, and he loved to point out just how smart he was to anyone who would tolerate him. In spite of this, he fit in with the others and wasn't always a dick. His brains came in handy in basic training when their problem-solving tests, usually involving some horrendous weather condition or other mortal peril, were rapidly solved by his keen intellect.

"Well, both of your dumb asses are wrong," Leslie Brandt said from atop the next bunk over, "because you're both missing the bigger picture."

It was Jake and Jamie's turn to roll their eyes.

"Yeah, yeah, we know," Jake said to try and stem the wave of propaganda he knew that she was about to spew out. "There's more to life than our own selfish desires, think about the planet as a whole, what we can do for humanity, yadda yadda…" He paused as he saw Brandt's eyes narrow at him.

"I'm just saying that you two should think about it," she said flatly. "There's nothing wasted about a life spent in service."

"So, what?" Jamie asked her. "You're going to spend a year and a half on this frozen rock, then go home and sign on the dotted line again? For good? *Forever?*"

"Maybe," she said hesitantly. "It's the only way to get fast-tracked."

Jake rested his face in his hands, although slowly and surreptitiously so as not to invite her wrath. She had been drunk on the UNPF's propaganda ever since she'd earned the single white stripe over her right shoulder during their long training period. Although she still ate, slept and trained with the rest of the squad, they knew that she had designs far above the lowly rank of petty officer class two.

Fast-track meant that she would have to undergo a program of high-stress testing, would have each of her mission and training progress reports picked apart and would have to jump through a dozen other hoops before they accepted her. If they did, if by some miracle she made it through, then she would have signed her entire life into service with the UNPF in return for a speedy promotion course to the rank of commander. She wouldn't get the same perks that the others did, wouldn't get the additional pay bump to be received tax-free when they got back to Earth after an overseas tour with CTSF off-world, but she would be rewarded with a grueling training program which would see her rise through the officer ranks quickly.

"Alright, assholes," the harsh voice of Master Petty Officer Carter announced as he stalked into the room. His words had the desired effect, as though someone had bawled for them to stand to attention. The two squads lined up at the foot of their bunks.

He walked tall, still wearing his armor, only minus the helmet now, whereas most of the squad members had at least stripped off the heavy chest and back plates.

"Guard and Recon," Carter said, addressing them by their unofficial names dictated by their specialized roles.

Jake, Jamie and Leslie's was the Recon squad, and they were trained for exactly that, whereas the Guard squad was more into heavy weapons. The other six squads of their unit, numbered three to eight, would be doubled-up in identical barracks on the same gray corridor in the same dull barracks that seemed to be designed the same way no matter the location in the inhabited galaxy.

"PO2s and ensigns by the door as usual. Don't screw about and in return I promise I won't make it my personal mission to rearrange your internals. Rectally." Carter paused to eyeball the nearest seaman, daring him to hold the contact. "Mission briefing in thirty, so strip and stow your gear." With that, he turned to stalk out of the room. The young lieutenant hot on his heels was too scared of the man to offer confrontational confirmation that he outranked him.

A chorus of 'aye, aye,' echoed after them before the normal buzz of chatter resumed.

The lieutenants, each in charge of a pair of ten-man squads, would have separate quarters. They would be sharing, as would the petty officer class one ranks, but from there on up, rank held the privilege of privacy. The master POs, usually called 'Boss' by the seamen under their command—calling someone *master* had a number of different and often awkward connotations to it—would have their own small quarters. Those ranks had the responsibility of over half of the unit each and reported to the two men who really ran the show.

The unit's commander, a man named Dassiova, was a hard-bitten soldier who was the veteran of a number of Earth conflicts and was widely renowned as one of the best. Rumor had it that he had been offered promotion back to Earth half a dozen times, going back to an elevated command position or an admiralship or else to take charge of training at one of the biggest academies, and each time he had refused. Dassiova preferred to stay at the sharp edge of UNPF service. This was his third lunar tour, his first since returning from another stint on the Close Protection teams, UNPF's elite Special Operations teams. Although he was one of the most highly respected UNPF unit commanders there was, their command chief and senior NCO was all that and then some.

"Fast-track or not," Jake said when the room had returned to normal, "I'll be glad to get back home and not have to trust domes and shield units to stop my eyeballs from being sucked out into space while my body flash-freezes."

He turned, slapping a hand twice on his shoulder for Paterson to unclip the heavy armor. The equipment had been designed to be put on and taken off by the user alone, but that user had to be double-jointed to do it without injuring themselves.

Brandt said nothing as she stowed her own armor in the locker. The lockers must have been specifically and intentionally designed to be only ninety percent big enough to hold their gear.

She pulled on her uniform jacket, brushing out the creases caused by being rolled up in her bag on the journey up from Earth, and clipped on the duty belt with its empty sidearm holster and pouches. Fully armored or not, none of them would be carrying a weapon until issued with them by the lunar armory master petty officer.

"Ready in fifteen," she said, raising her voice for her squad of ten seamen to mutter their aye, ayes.

"Isn't that the wheel's job?" Jake asked her, his voice just loud enough for the sixteen-year-old ensign to hear.

They were called 'wheels' by everyone after an old saying about something useless being the fifth wheel. However, seeing as all of their vehicles were at least six-wheeled the saying had lost its meaning. The wheel himself, Kyle Torres, pretended not to hear the seaman's slight at his expense and carried on unpacking his gear. The top bunk he had been relegated to, the one nearest the door so that he could supposedly keep an eye on the comings and goings of his squad, seemed too high for him to reach without clambering up the end of the frame like a child.

"Can it, Santana," Brandt told Jake, trying not to smile.

CHAPTER 2

UNPF Barracks, Lunar Base

"The terrorism threat level remains at severe," Commander Dassiova growled from the dais, "but we are not here as an overt armed force. Our task is to patrol, engage, gather any relevant intelligence and pass that back up the chain of command. Full battle armor will be maintained at all times but stowed in barracks, and only sidearms and stun batons will be issued. Now, for the sake of not doing too many goddamned administrative duties, these weapons will be personal issue and will not be recalled at the end of duty shifts, *but*," he paused to glare at the entire assembled unit, "if anyone, and I mean *anyone* decides to misuse, misplace one or in any way cause me to hear your name in a sentence that involves anything other than your sterling effort and gleaming hard work, then I will personally guarantee you will find yourselves *walking* back to Earth at the end of your tour. And that is if you're lucky. Chief?"

The commander stepped back, taking his small sheaf of paperwork and looking just as pissed off as everyone else was to be babysitting a boring-but-potentially-hostile environment. He'd rather be fully armored and tooled-up ready for anything. The command chief petty officer was a bull of a man standing at a flat six feet tall, and with more presence than should be humanly possible. He was a legend in the UNPF and had been one of the NCOs traded between territories a decade earlier as part of the cross-training plans to standardize the Earth's security forces.

Originally from Nigeria, Afamefuna Onyilogwu found it much easier to go by his title of 'Chief' and was rumored to have issued a significant amount of punishment to those junior ranks who attempted to pronounce his surname and failed. Those junior ranks included, if rumor was to be believed, a number of lieutenant commanders.

"Listen up, people," he snapped. "We will do this by the numbers. Squad lieutenants have your duty rotations and areas of responsibility. All of you will eventually learn these areas as well as those on either side of your own. Our standard of interaction is to be friendly and courteous, and only to resort to force if verbal commands are not obeyed."

He looked around the assembled squad, somehow managing to eyeball every one of the eighty seamen, fourteen NCOs and fourteen officers deemed to be under the level of himself and the commander. "This I will repeat, just in case any of you are feeling a little hard of hearing: We do not use force unless we have to, and nobody will discharge their sidearm unless they are being shot at, is that clear?"

A loud collective shout of *aye, aye* blasted the room and Chief waited for silence once more.

"And one last thing, anyone caught using the stun batons on one another in the barracks will personally answer to me."

The quiet threat sucked the oxygen out of the room as quickly as if a seal had cracked on the large dome they were under.

Squad by squad, they filed out of the briefing area in reverse order, leaving the Recon squad last out. They waited for their turn to shuffle toward the armory and be given their standard issue 6mm Universal Service Pistols as well as the stun batons. They were more excited about the batons in the childish and mischievous way Chief had expected. There was a running bet going around each squad as to who would be the first to mess up and shock themselves, and Chief's warning underlined the fact that walls had ears.

Their use of firearms was heavily limited because almost half of the lunar colony was still protected from the vacuum of space by physical double-skinned domes and not the new large forcefields generated by the latest generation of singularity energy sources. These forcefield domes could withstand a heavy supersonic round from their 12mm Squad Support Weapons, but the physical domes were at risk from anything bigger than the 6mm subsonic ammunition. Their main weapon, the imaginatively named Universal Service Rifle was a bullpup carbine firing the same caliber of ammunition as the pistols but with an option to increase the charge and fire the round supersonically. Those rounds could, in theory, penetrate the dome, which is why their guns remained locked up tightly.

"What area have we got, Les?" Jake asked.

"Pipe down and get a grip," she told him. "You'll find out when you find out."

Paterson caught Jake's eye and the two exchanged a knowing look.

Get a grip? She doesn't know either.

They waited, their lieutenant calling them calmly to wait in line to scan their hands against the greasy tablet in exchange for a stubby sidearm, three spare magazines, and lastly, their telescopic baton. They had to stand inside a marked safety area and draw it to make sure it crackled into life, before demonstrating that they could safely collapse it and stop the flow of sixty thousand volts. After that, they went down the line to the loading area where they loaded their three magazines, and placed one into the weapon ahead of the pistol grip.

Next, they pointed them into the heavy rubber curtains in front of the big drums filled with the dust from the Moon's surface meant to smother any errant discharge. They applied their safety catches, showed the petty officer in charge of the station, and holstered the guns.

Jake, unique among his squad and often mocked for being left handed, quickly went through the practiced process of breaking down the weapon to switch the ejection port from right to left, before replacing the top slide and loading his weapon.

Getting back to their barracks and looking around to make sure nobody senior was present, they drew their stun batons and pushed their luck as far as they dared by feigning tasering each other.

"Officer on deck!" barked the petty officer class one in charge of the two squads in the barrack room. As one, they snapped to attention, running to stand by the end of their beds and pretend they weren't playing with their newly issued weaponry. The lieutenant walked in, no doubt having sent the NCO ahead to make sure that nobody was witnessed disobeying Chief's standing orders, then called for the ensigns and NCOs from each squad to form on him.

Santana and Paterson strained to overhear the orders, without success. The lieutenant left with his NCO, and Leslie returned to Recon squad where the others gathered around her.

"Our area," said a small voice from halfway behind her, "is lunar spaceport arrivals." All eyes turned to the young ensign, Torres, and he seemed to deflate slightly under their combined gaze. Unsure of himself, he glanced up to Brandt.

"Twelve-hour rotations," she said. "We've scored the day shift working six 'til six. Guard Squad get the night shift. We do that for six days at a time, then we get seventy-two hours stand-down. That means we are off duty now until muster at oh-four-hundred for PT and biscuits. Briefing at oh-five-forty-five. Questions?"

"What's our remit?" asked a seaman to her left.

"We are on customs and search," she said. "We'll rotate, but we'll have three on cargo search under the command of Ensign Torres, the rest of you are on patrol and inbound-outbound checks. Brush up on your search techniques tonight."

"Where's O-O-B?" Paterson asked.

"Technically nothing is out of bounds," Brandt said, "but you will all stick to the barracks compound: head, gym, mess hall, and crash deck. Let us get a grip of things and we'll see about shore leave."

The crash deck, as they called it, was their designated area for enlisted men and women to relax off-duty. It was bad etiquette for officers and senior NCOs—master petty officers and above—to invite themselves in, but the payoff was that the enlisted ranks kept the place clean and didn't do anything so raucous as to warrant their presence.

The squad melted away to finish stowing their gear and try to fit the square pegs in the round holes, given their too-small lockers. In the end, a requisition for two dozen footlockers was made and rapidly approved, dispelling the myth of UNPF administrative bureaucracy taking over a month to approve more toilet paper. They ate, the food being just as awful as Jake had predicted, then hung around to check out the facilities, before hitting their bunks in the half-empty room as Guard Squad had already left for their night shift.

Four in the morning came far too quickly, leaving many of them with the feeling of not having been asleep long enough to conduct a day's work. PT was led by one of the squad, as it was one of her two trained specialisms. It was a quiet affair but still got them sweating. Something about the unnatural atmosphere and the artificial gravity made them feel sluggish. They jogged laps around the large gymnasium, counting down their number and shouting it as they passed the start line until they reached five miles. As they ran, Santana and Paterson talked.

"You seen one of those new shield domes yet?" Jake asked, knowing that if anyone would know about them, his academic friend would.

"Yeah, just not on this scale. You know they're actually terraforming under them? The shields cover, like, thirty miles in each direction and can hold it for a hundred years. Probably longer. Not that it'll wear off or anything because they'll just replace the singularity drives powering it."

The singularity drives were what had caused things to improve for the human race, though at first they had made things get a whole lot worse. The discovery of a clean, renewable and incredibly powerful energy source had ended humanity's reliance on fossil fuels. The world erupted into war almost overnight and the United Nations had extended its power using the new technology until order was restored to humanity. That left four main territories under a centralized government. The dominant territory, if there was such a thing, was the entire amalgamated American continent, and when the human race finally decided to work together, they achieved great things. All that was way back in the past though, even before their grandparents' time.

"You wait," Jake said. "One day they'll figure out how to make them small enough to fit to our armor instead of just the ships and planets. That'll be a game changer."

"And you think they'd rush to deliver that new tech to us grunts on the front line?"

Jake thought about it. "Probably not. But, hey, it's not like I'll still be driving a suit when that eventually happens."

The Moon had been first colonized over eighty years earlier, but the new wave of technological advances was being implemented and the surface was being transformed into a version of their own home planet, using the shield domes to create large circles of atmosphere.

Eventually two massive shield generators were supposed to be built on the opposing poles of the Moon. Once they were turned on, the entire moon would be sealed and allow for a breathable atmosphere to be created. That was after at least fifty years of terraforming and pumping oxygen and nitrogen into the space where there used to be nothing. Each flight brought more scientists and more hydroponic equipment up to the surface to begin transforming the barren surface into something entirely new.

"Cut the chatter," barked their PT. "You got air to talk, you got air to run faster!"

The men kept their chatter to a minimum, continuing their conversation at a level that didn't invite the reward of extra push-ups.

"You reckon they'll make the Moon green like Earth?" Jake whispered.

"No real reason why not," Paterson answered. "There's frozen glaciers here, and as long as the domes don't fail, then there's every chance they can sorta *grow* an atmosphere underneath. It just has to happen in—*forty-two*—" they yelled together as they passed the start line again, "—stages."

"But how do they get around the fact that the days are two weeks long here? And how do they stop the air, you know, *leaking out*?"

"A geodesic dome structure sits underneath the actual shield and creates the artificial day and night," Paterson explained, the scientist part of him overtaking the cocky grunt persona he hid behind every day. "The shielding is the same as the domes in that they actually extend pretty far underground."

"I thought you were some physics dude?" Jake asked him, "Not into all this terraforming stuff…"

"*Dude*," Paterson told him, mocking his Californian accent, "read a datapad…"

At forty-six they stopped, dropping into push-ups and sit-ups in pairs. Jake and Jamie earned an extra ten of each to prove that their PT had known it was they who had been talking.

"Alright," Brandt said as they formed up to file out of the gymnasium while Squad Four waited to file in. "Showers and mess hall for biscuits."

Biscuits, for reasons none of them understood, were what they called breakfast in the UNPF. Given their maritime roots, some believed it was a derivative of ship's biscuits, but either way it was more bland food that did nothing for Jake's high-maintenance taste buds. Paterson joked that his mother's cooking had spoiled him, and now nothing the UNPF could serve him came close to her home-cooked recipes. They dressed in their uniforms, holstered their batons and pistols, and moved to report to the lunar docks for duty. Pausing in the doorway of their barracks, Paterson called for the attention of his two friends.

"Hold up," he said. He produced his datapad from his locker and swiped the screen to show a wobbling image of him, Jake and Brandt.

"Say cheese, dumbasses," she said as they all grinned at the camera for the last image they would ever have of them all together.

Santana and Paterson both smiled up at the camera, and just as Brandt said cheese they chorused, *"Get a grip!"*

CHAPTER 3

Crash Deck, Lunar Barracks

"We are The Choosers," said the digitized voice from the speakers built into the large screen, "and we choose not to be a part of the heresy and recklessness of the United Nations and their godless forays into space." The face, obscured by computerized trickery, leaned closer to the camera. "Your reign of sovereignty is at an end, and the people of Earth will no longer stand for you making our decisions for us.

"You colonized the Moon when we objected, but you did not stop. You subject our brothers and sisters to death, torture and internment and still you do not stop. Now you want to take more of humanity to Mars and colonize there." The shrouded face leaned back, and the intense voice lessened into something calm and frightening. "If you do not stop, you will invite the destruction of our species. You will announce our presence to the rest of the universe and our galaxy will be invaded by outsiders, by alien races with technology far superior to our own. It will be the end for humanity."

"Fuck you, asshole!" shouted one of the men pointlessly from Squad Five who had clearly drunk more than the three permitted beverages for an off-duty seaman. Murmurs of agreement rippled through the crash deck and broke the silence as they stared at the large screen. The terrorist leaders who claimed responsibility for the attack on the lunar space port were broadcasting planet-wide.

"Choosers? More like *losers*!" drawled a grunt who was leaning heavily against a wall, drawing out the last word in an attempt at comedy.

"We did not choose to colonize space," the synthesized voice said, "and you will no longer be permitted to choose for the rest of us."

With that, the screen flashed black for a second before the exquisitely groomed anchorwoman returned to view with her best somber look on display. Her normally brightly colored dress had been replaced by one a deep blue so dark it seemed black, and behind her played scenes of burning wreckage being doused by fire-suppressant drones.

"That was the message from the terrorist group calling themselves The Choosers, and tonight Global Television Networks received the following message from the organization known as The Freedom to Choose, which some say is the parent organization of those who carried out the attack." She glanced away from the camera to watch the clip about to be played on screen.

"I am a representative of the peaceful group, The Freedom to Choose. We are not associated with the terrorists who call themselves The Choosers, and we condemn their cowardly attack on the lunar base. The slaughter of innocents is not the way to have valid political concerns heard, and we are in no way responsible for this tragic and senseless loss of life. Our thoughts and prayers are with those affected tonight."

"That's a load of bull," came a growl from near the back of the room. "Half of *those* assholes are what started the *other* assholes." A murmur of agreement rippled around the room, dropping the temperature of the mood even further. What the man had said was true though; The Choosers or The Freedom made no difference. They were, or at least had been at some point, one and the same.

The only difference now was that some of them wanted to sit around talking about fighting back and others wanted to fight instead of talking. It was a pointless scenario with no end in sight.

"Officer on deck!" bawled the unmistakable voice of Chief, snapping the entire crash deck to their feet, where they stood to attention.

He walked in, eyeing half of the men and women of his unit who had pulled daytime duty and making it silently obvious that he knew more than a few of them were swaying in an imaginary breeze. Behind him, shorter and wearing a mask of poorly veiled hate, came the commander, who was followed by the puffy red face of Ensign Torres.

"At ease," he said almost reluctantly. "CTSF have sent a relief unit to take over our duties here as of oh-nine-thirty tomorrow. Until that time, the squads on duty will remain on station."

The whole of the lunar base had been locked down, and any ship either waiting to dock or in transit to the Moon had been turned away. One of those claimed a medical emergency, so a UNPF shuttle flew out to dock with them and offload the casualty. The crew opted to remain in orbit. Nothing would come in or out until the relief force arrived to take military command of the entire base. Many of them thought that perhaps the UN wanted something like the terror attacks to happen, so they could be justified in taking full control of the planet from the civilian contingent.

Dassiova turned to leave, Chief glowering over the swaying heads of the grunts and daring one of them to speak.

"Recon squad," the commander said loudly enough to be heard at the back of the room, "or what's left of you, muster on me."

The assembled faces turned to locate the nearest member of Recon with a mixture of fear, jealousy and pity showing in their expressions. None of them knew what they were being summoned for, but all of them felt like they had suffered enough loss, stress and pain for one day.

"Alright," Brandt said as she tried to control her voice and her emotions after her second tequila chaser had started to take effect. "Sober up, buttercups. Let's do this."

She'd had the two small bullet holes in her flank sealed with dermal plugs, pretty much battlefield surgery as the Moon's main med bay was inundated with so many injuries caused by the gunfight and the panic. They had scanned her eyes, told her she didn't have a concussion and gave her three days' worth of painkillers and a single stim pack to get her going. Despite it being a bad idea, she went to drink with her unit instead of getting the prescribed bed rest.

She led the contingent of four out of the door, six seamen and the lieutenant who had been on the day shift absent as they lay in body bags in the freezer. Six, including the young wheel, out of thirteen. Almost half of their squad lost inside of five minutes. At least they had killed all twelve of the terrorists, and managed to stop the device from going off. Off-duty seamen from Squad Three had been roused to disarm and defuse the bomb, because none of the surviving members of Recon were demolitions trained. All five of them were on their way to being drunk, and not even the sobering fear of an impending interaction with Chief and the commander was straightening their footsteps as they followed in line to the briefing room.

"Sit down and shut up," Chief said in a tone that was marginally less hostile and full of hate than he usually employed. It lured them into thinking that perhaps he was trying to be sympathetic. They sat down in silence. Only the two heads of the unit and the ensign were there until a fourth and fifth person walked in. Both wore fashionable business suits: matte black and tightly fitted up to the collarless neck. Both seemed athletic but not overtly muscled, and the one at

31

the back seemed oddly androgynous. Both had haircuts that spoke of military service, high and tight, but something about them said they danced to a different tune, one that was far better funded than their service appeared to be.

"These people are here on invitation of the UN Intelligence Directorate," Commander Dassiova said. "As you had the closest contact with the terrorists they will take your statements about the attack."

"Sir?" Brandt said, made brave by the tequila. She stood to attention to address her commanding officer, who glared at her.

"What is it, PO?"

"Sir, we've already written our reports and submitted them."

Chief stepped forward, no doubt winding up to deliver a nuclear-grade ass-chewing for questioning the commander, before he was stopped by a quiet word from one of the two suited figures.

"True," one of them said as she stepped forward. The plain suit and military haircut had masked the truth of her gender. "And we have read them, but we want to speak to you further. After that, you will be…"

"*After that,*" the commander growled to cut her off, "you will receive orders." He said nothing further, just glanced at Chief, who stood them to attention and followed him out of the room. Chief glanced back, exchanging a subtle nod with the suited man that was so fleeting Brandt suspected she might have imagined it.

One by one they were taken into another room by both suits. They were attached to a machine like an old-fashioned polygraph. Their vitals were displayed on a tablet that was turned around after they had seen it. Brandt guessed that was deliberate so that she, as the subject, had an idea about what they were measuring. The green light blinked on the back of the tablet facing her and she guessed the camera was active, dialed in to focus on her pupil response.

She recited her name, rank, service number and details of her family address back on Earth before she was asked about siblings and parents. She realized this could establish her baseline responses from facts that were easy to check.

They went over her report, line by line and asking for verbal confirmation of the truth of each statement, before extracting a little more detail every time.

"Seaman Jake Santana," the androgynous female operative said, smirking slightly as Brandt's eyes and vital signs betrayed her and gave an honest response. She knew she had responded, because she felt her cheeks flush.

"What about him?" she asked, a little too much hostility in her tone, which she tried to apportion to the alcohol.

"Tell me about him."

Brandt set her jaw to stop her lower lip from trembling. She blinked a few times trying to hide the tears that pricked at her eyes, but she couldn't keep them away. She bowed her head, hands rising to wipe away the water from her cheeks, then fixed the operative asking the questions with the full force of her gaze.

"Seaman. Combat and Electronic Countermeasure specialist."

"And?"

"And he's dead. I spent almost every day of the last three and a half years with him, fought, trained and lived beside him, and now he's gone."

"Did you see anything abnormal about the terrorist who killed him?"

Brandt hesitated, unsure whether to say what she really saw, but her anger and frustration made her speak.

"I saw Jake shoot him point-blank with an entire mag and he stayed on his feet. That was pretty abnormal, I'd say."

The operative hesitated, glancing at her counterpart who nodded.

"We found Seaman Santana's personal weapon," she said unconvincingly. "It seems to have malfunctioned and not fired."

Brandt's expression showed that she thought that was bullshit of the highest order, but it never paid to call out people when you didn't know who they were or who they reported to.

"Have you told anyone else what you think you saw?"

Brandt thought. Lying would be pointless and counterproductive, so she told the truth.

"I discussed it with Paterson. He saw the same thing."

"Do you think Santana is a hero?" the operative asked, eyes still down to the pad and startling her with the change of direction.

"What they hell is your problem?" Brandt snarled. "Of course he's a goddamned hero. Get a grip. Why wouldn't he be? He died stopping that bomb from going off and now you want to do what? A post-mission performance evaluation? Go to hell." She stood, pulling the sensors from her hands and tangling in the legs of the chair. As she untangled herself, she winced and clasped a hand to the fused wounds in her side that still hurt.

"I think he's a hero," the operative said quietly, stopping her in her tracks. "I just wanted to be sure that you all thought that too."

~

Their debrief took them late into the night, and Brandt was sober again by the time the surviving members of her squad had been through the same questioning. Their wheel, Torres, had fallen asleep across two chairs in the briefing room. He was curled up like a kid and she had ordered the others to pipe down so they didn't wake the young officer.

He's been through enough, she thought. *Last thing he needs is more hazing from these jerks.*

In the end he was woken with a start anyway, as Chief stalked in without warning to startle them all to their feet.

"Stand easy," he told them quietly, respectful of the hour and how long they had been on their feet. "I have your orders. Ensign Torres, Petty Officer Class Two Brandt, Seaman Paterson: you are on a shuttle back to Earth departing in twenty. Your kit has already been cleared out except your suits and stowed aboard. You three," he said as he turned his attention to the three surviving seamen, "you will join other squads to replace sickness."

"Chief," Brandt said, her voice loud and confident, "with respect, why are we being benched when there's still work to do here?"

Chief looked at her, his mouth forming a shape like a rumbling volcano about to erupt, but he calmed and answered her interruption with civility.

"You are not being benched," he told her. "You have been tasked with escorting a science team back to Earth and then you will report to OTA Colima. And don't *ever* 'with respect' me again."

Brandt opened her mouth to respond but no words came out. She shut her mouth again and opened it as though she had changed her mind, but the look on Chief's face made it clear that she should say nothing. She glanced at Paterson, his own eyes willing her to shut up and take it, because it looked like she was being given exactly what she wanted.

Officer Training Academy? she thought. *But I only put that in my last appraisal as a potential career move. I haven't even applied.*

They walked back to the barracks in a daze. The two seamen were grumbling about being reassigned and asking Paterson why he got to go home. Paterson ignored them, as did Brandt and the ensign.

They climbed into their armor suits in silence, using the buddy system to secure the individual parts in a group of three and ignoring the sullen looks from the other grunts on their way to new accommodation for the next eighteen months. True to Chief's word, the rest of their personal kit was gone. Two petty officers arrived and issued them with new weapons, this time their standard carbines as well as new pistols, and handed over the spare magazines which were clipped into place on the outside of their armor.

"Orders from the admiral," one said, handing over a communication module to each of them, which clipped onto their left forearms.

"The admiral?" Torres asked, his small features looking lost at sea from inside the gunmetal gray suit. They looked down to their orders in turn.

"OTA Colima," Torres said quietly. "Lieutenant's course. But I'm not due to take that unless I sign on for another five years. I've only served one."

"Same for me," Brandt said, her eyes wide in shock. She turned her forearm over, the display flipping upside down to show the others her orders.

Torres whistled softly.

"Fast track?" Paterson asked.

"Yeah," Brandt said in shock, turning the screen back to her.

"But I have to sign on for life if I do that. What about you?" Paterson showed his own orders. A full scholarship to any college of his choosing, sponsored by the UNPF.

"I get to go to college, paid for by the UN, apparently." Brandt's eyes narrowed.

"Does this check five-oh to you?" she asked, asking if the others thought something fishy was going on.

"You mean that the three of us survive something and end up getting everything we want when the others have to go back to work? Yeah. Something ain't right," Paterson agreed.

"Who cares?" Torres asked. "Earth chow and no more rations. Promotions for us. You get yourself free college place," he added to Paterson. "I say we don't look too hard at it."

CHAPTER 4

Lunar Departures

"You Brandt?" the helmetless man in the last generation powered armor asked as they approached the shuttle. Brandt glanced at the young officer, almost annoyed on his behalf at being ignored now that she was facing the realistic prospect of being a wheel in some other unit soon.

"Yeah," she said. "This is Lieutenant Torres."

The man looked to Torres, the single star and his very young face not matching up with the rank she had just given him.

"Well alrighty then," he said with an unconcerned smile, his southern accent almost mocking in its informality. "Looks like you're the security detail's security detail."

Her face must have registered confusion as he explained further.

"We're with Hyper," he said, indicting two other men in similar armor. Their weapons were the same as the ones the UNPF issued, only they weren't stenciled with the same markings and appeared well worn. The two other men looked at them like cats watching mice. "We're dropping planetside, and we get off with the eggheads." He jerked his head over his other shoulder at the science team who were fussing over two large black cases they moved on repulser jets. They tapped at the interactive screen on the lid of one as it moved, chattering away to each other in intense murmurs.

Brandt had heard of Hyper. They had all heard of Hyper. They heard they were developing tech faster than the combined territories were. The Hudson-Yu Progression & Research group, or HYPR, was a multi-national business with manufacturing and research plants in all of the four territories.

"Well, anyways," the man said. "The name's Horne. Your gear is already stowed, so grab yourself a seat."

The engines started and the cargo ramp closed. They must have been waiting for the three UN personnel. They sat, stowing their weapons by the numbers and strapping in before they put their helmets on and pressurized their suits to see the world via the HUDs inside their visors. Cruel, mocking laughter was fed to their ears from the sensors and speakers, and they looked at the three private military contractors who were lounging in unassigned seating still with their helmets off and strapped to the hooks on their belts. They clearly found the adherence to protocol to be funny, just like the wasters in school who mocked the smart kids for trying hard and doing their homework.

Something about their demeanor made Brandt angry, but whether it was their arrogance or just the fact that they seemed sloppy and undisciplined she didn't know. She sat back, her visor mirroring to the command she tapped into her forearm communication and control unit, and waited for the journey to end.

About an hour in, she woke, her mind taking a few seconds to adapt and tell her where she was. She recalled, with horrifying clarity, recent events before she recognized the sounds that had brought her back to consciousness.

It was panic. Controlled panic with low voices but it was still panic.

"We're losing him," one of the scientists complained as he tapped furiously with two fingers on the control screen of one of the black crates lashed to the deck.

"Increase to three-sixty and go again," said another. "No response. Charging again."

A dull noise sounded from inside the crate. "Rhythm," another one said. "It's weak."

"Twenty cc's epinephrine," said the lead scientist, his one hand held behind his back as the other gripped a safety handle on the bulkhead.

"Rate increasing... back inside normal parameters... holding."

They seemed to relax, having averted whatever disaster had challenged them. Brandt unclipped herself and stood, taking two paces toward the scientists until Horne and his two cronies rose to block her path. One of them, she now saw, had a small, black case cuffed to his left wrist.

"Can't let you do that, Chief," he said apologetically, his face showing reluctance and deference but his eyes not smiling to match.

"Stand aside, civilian," Brandt said, hoping to bully her way past with the loudspeaker of her suit making her sound bigger.

"Not going to happen," Horne answered equably. "You have your orders. I have mine. And mine say that nobody touches those crates or those scientists. Stand down, please."

Torres and Paterson both rose to flank Brandt as soon as the stand-off began, but even she had to admit that the three private military contractors had the edge even without their helmets on. Nobody had drawn a weapon, nobody had even stood up to their full height yet, but the impasse was palpable. It was like when two predators met in the open back on Earth, and instead of fighting and risking injury or death they did their best to look intimidating and scare the other one off so that they thought tangling with them was more hassle than it was worth.

"Come on, Brandt," Paterson said. "Don't let the toy soldiers piss on your boots."

Brandt allowed him to pull her back, glancing over Horne's shoulder at the nearest of the black crates and the unconcerned scientists ignoring them.

"That's right," crooned one of the men behind Horne, making the man roll his eyes with embarrassment, "y'all go ahead and run along now."

"They've got people in there," she said to her friends. She had opened a private channel to their suit designations and spoke privately thanks to the sealed armor. "Injured people. That was a resuscitation they just did."

"Who do you think it is?" Torres asked.

"I don't know," Brandt answered, "as far as I knew all the terrorists were dead. Same as our guys."

"Well, we ain't gonna figure it out," Paterson told them as he tapped at his own module to increase the internal heat by a few degrees to help him sleep. "May as well just enjoy my last goddamned ride in space."

~

Their re-entry was rough, like it often was, and this time not even Paterson could sleep through it. The shuttle made more noise when inside the Earth's atmosphere, and the high-pitched chirping whistle of the singularity-driven engine was audible through their sensor feeds. Brandt was torn between keeping their communication secret and getting out of the claustrophobic helmet, and in the end her need for freedom won. Unclipping the hissing helmet away from her bulky suit she dialed in the communication device to the ship channel.

"Roger," crooned the pilot. "Approach vector one-six-eight on descent, requesting docking platform."

"Lunar four-eight-four, you are cleared for landing pad nineteen. Confirm?"

"Confirm pad one-niner, ETA six minutes. Four-eight-four standing by."

Brandt caught the eyes of Ensign Torres, holding up all of the digits of her right hand and her left thumb. He nodded back, elbowing Paterson and showing him six fingers. He nodded, unclipping his helmet and wiping his damp face. The higher temperature he had set was marginally too much for the suit to recycle. That was a flaw with their armor units—nobody ever stayed cool and calm when in a fight and Peterson had been warned more than once about messing with the settings on his armor.

They waited, eager to get out of their suits. Unfortunately, they'd have to be at their end destination before stripping off the heavy plates again otherwise they wouldn't be able to carry them.

The shuttle banged down, gas struts creaking as their landing gear compressed, and the tail ramp lowered with a metallic whine. Two teams of white-coated personnel waited, and the team onboard rushed their black crates down the ramp to each team as one gave a verbal report.

"This one coded four hours ago," he said. "Stable now but we need to prep for surgery right away. Is Doctor Hamada here yet?"

Brandt unclipped to stand, hoping to wander around outside for at least a minute before they had to take off again, but Horne stopped her with his right hand. His left was behind his back carrying the same case she had seen earlier cuffed to his wrist.

"Sorry, Chief," he said, deliberately inflating her status in another attempt to disarm her. "This is a restricted area. Hyper personnel only." He walked backward down the ramp, a cocky swagger in his steps as his boots hit solid ground and the tail ramp whirred up again. Before his face went out of sight, he winked.

"Argh," Brandt said in exasperation. "Screw those guys."

Any answer was cut off by an announcement from the pilot.

"Taking off for the American territory now, ETA seven-nine minutes."

Brandt sat back, trying to force the unanswered questions out of her head.

The shuttle landed at OTA Colima, the UN American Territory's officer training academy in Mexico, and the wall of heat hit them before the ramp had even fully descended.

All three of them tapped at their suit controls to manually change the internal temperature. The software that detected and adjusted it took somewhere between a minute and roughly four months to catch up.

"Looks like this is you two," Paterson said with a sad smile. He offered his hand to the young ensign, the boy who was soon to become Lieutenant Torres, and shook it warmly.

"You were a good wheel," he told him. "You didn't get in the way."

"Asshole," Torres said warmly, smiling at the man who had been in battle with him for the first time, no matter how brief it had been.

43

Torres checked his holstered weapons, hoisted his bag, which was almost the same size as he was, and walked down the ramp into the scorching sunlight. Brandt turned to Paterson and looked hard into his eyes.

"Go get your degree, and do something useful with it," she told him. "Maybe invent something awesome and retire." In answer, he stood to attention and saluted in a fashion she thought sarcastic.

"Ma'am, yes ma'am," he said, half in jest.

"Asshole," she said as she hugged him and clanked their armor together.

CHAPTER 5

Sapporo Mountains, Japan

The science team left the landing pad before the shuttle had even taken off again as the man in charge barked orders. Doctor Hamada, unusually tall for a native of the island they were on, headed up the bioengineering division at what had once been the Yu Foundation headquarters, but was now the research center for the Hudson-Yu company. A medical doctor by trade, a gifted surgeon and leader in the development of neurologically controlled prosthetic limb replacements, his work had long been submerged in the murky world of weapons and cybernetics enhancement research.

"The human body is a remarkable thing," he said to the team pushing the hovering crates along in his wake as he strode purposefully ahead. "It is capable of surviving the most horrific injuries, but even I cannot repair the damage if you do not *hurry up*." His last words descended into a snarl at the doctors and technicians bustling along behind him. He said nothing more as glass and steel doors hissed open ahead of him at the command of a uniformed and armed guard behind them. He stripped off his white lab coat as he walked and dropped it on the ground knowing that someone else would pick it up, have it cleaned and restored to the closet in his office along with all the contents of his pockets finding their neat way to his antique desk.

He walked through another set of doors to his right, these opening automatically as the crates and the teams pushing them went straight ahead through another opening. He stopped, stepping out of his clothes unashamedly as he was handed a clean set of scrubs, which he stepped into with practiced ease.

Slipping his feet into a sterile set of rubber shoes, he scrubbed-in, working his hands and forearms meticulously but quickly. Standing and shaking his hands dry he put both arms into a machine that sparked to life and blasted the skin with light particles, before backing through a manual set of doors with his hands held clear of his body. He turned and had sterile gloves placed over his hands and a mask looped over his ears.

"I think something classic today," he said amiably to a technician in full surgical get-up. The young man turned and tapped at the icons on a screen and the speakers built into the walls began to play music. As the haunting tones and repetitive thudding beat of the twenty-first century dance music filled the room, Hamada smiled beneath his mask and bobbed his head appreciatively. "Nothing like the old school for a job like this," he said. "Now, who do we have here?"

The black crate, scrubbed clean with charged light beams and devoid of the team that had escorted it from the surface of the Moon, floated toward him.

"Massive limb damage," another doctor said as she read the facts from the screen of a datapad held in front of her by another surgical assistant. "Pressurized damage to skull and scans indicate some kind of spinal swelling in the lower thoracic."

"So I've got a torso with brain damage and probable paralysis," Hamada complained.

"Seriously, what do these people expect of me?" He mimed slapping a hand to his forehead, stopping short so that he didn't have to re-scrub.

"I imagine they expect results," the assistant surgeon told him, "like you give them every time."

"True," Hamada said with a sideways smirk at her. "But… come *on*! How bad is the other one?"

The female surgeon looked at the tech holding the datapad and waited as they flipped the screen and swiped until turning it back around for her to view. She pulled a face.

"Ah. Two bullets lodged in the spine at C-five, T-two. Three more embedded in upper right lung, right trapezius and right scapula."

"Nice grouping," Hamada opined casually, as though the accuracy of the shooter was the primary information worth commenting on. "No, I think we will stick with this one. Okay, open it up."

A technician tapped the commands onto the glass top of the crate before stepping back. It hissed, pressurized gas escaping into the sterile environment of the operating theater.

Eyes peered inside as the air cleared from the cold atmosphere contained inside the crate, and the full horror of the task became more apparent.

"Oh," Hamada said when the chilled body with wires and tubes snaking from it was revealed. "Okay then… let's get him out and transferred onto our respirator. I always prefer ours to the mobile ones, and I need a full neuro display, please."

He turned away from the ruined remains being slid horizontally onto the surgical table. The anesthesiologist changed the levels of drugs being pumped through the tubes to put the body deeper under. The procedure went smoothly.

"Let's see about getting this man the full benefit of his UNPF medical insurance, shall we?" Hamada said as he turned around. He looked carefully at the blackened and shriveled remains of the man lying in startling contrast to the white sterility of the table.

"What did he do?" Hamada asked, eyes wide in surprise that the man was even still alive.

"Running away from a terrorist bomb, apparently," the female surgeon answered.

"Hmm," Hamada grunted, not answering her but musing about how to approach the problem. "Okay, left leg transfemoral amputation, right leg will have to be a transpelvic hemipelvectomy. Looks nasty in there so best to get it all out of the way."

He nodded to the technician holding the datapad up for him to see now, waiting for the screen to be swiped over to the next scan image. "Zoom in there? Okay, left arm transradial, looks like more than half of the forearm is good but right arm will have to be upper transhumeral unless the damage to the shoulder girdle is too severe. Zoom in again and rotate left please?" he added to the tech.

He watched the screen and pulled a face.

"Yes, I don't think we need to do a full shoulder disarticulation, but I may need to reinforce the skeleton in a later operation." He stepped away from the screen and rolled his shoulders. "Okay, people. Let's do this."

The music was turned up slightly, the synthesized tones wailing sweetly along with the female vocals, and Hamada went to work cutting away the burn damage to save the rest of the body.

48

Agoura Hills, California

Maria Fernanda Santana turned with wet hands away from the sink to shout a string of Spanish at her youngest son like a burst of machine gun fire.

Water dripped from Maria's finger as she wagged it, the five-year-old boy stood frozen to the spot until she had finished, for fear of incurring further wrath. She was a small woman, short and thin-framed, but she possessed a furnace within her, like all Latin women with five children spanning over two decades. Her husband, the second one, worked long shifts in a factory where they manufactured the carbon ceramic Kevlar polymer. Even when he was home he wasn't that helpful, but since her eldest son had left home almost four years ago after high school, things had actually gotten more difficult. They got less expensive, since the young man ate more than both she and her husband did, but his absence was noticed. There was a big gap between him and his four siblings—his own father had passed when he was very young, and his mother remarried years later. He had been old enough to walk her down the aisle in place of her own father.

Her other children spanned from their early teens to the five-year-old currently pinned down by her vocal suppressing fire, but he was released by the sound of the high-pitched engines screaming in to land in the street outside.

She stopped, straightened, and turned to look out of the window at the small gunmetal gray transporter settling in to land outside her house.

Her eyes narrowed until she made out the circular globe emblem of the United Nations.

Her eyes went wide, and a sob caught in her throat as her hand fluttered up to her mouth.

49

"*Ay, ay Dios mío...*" she muttered feebly. "*Ay Dios no, por favor no.*"

Two men got out of the transport. Both donned headgear and walked slowly and somberly up to the house. Maria stayed frozen in the kitchen, her breath coming in rapid gasps until the doorbell startled her into movement. She almost ran to the door, snatching it open and launching into a verbal attack on them.

"Don't tell me," she screamed. "Don't you dare try to tell this to me! I tell you, don't say this."

"Mrs. Santana?" one of the men asked in a bored voice. A piece of paper in his hand held the information he wanted because he glanced down to it. "Ma'am, are you the mother of Seaman Jake Diego Santana currently assigned to the Combined Territories lunar defense units?"

Maria said nothing, just collapsed slowly to the ground sobbing. The two uniformed men looked at one another.

"Ma'am," the other one said, "on behalf of the President of the American Territory, you have our deepest condolences and it is with great regret that we must inform you of your son's passing."

Maria made no answer, but in recognition of the words she heard, the wailing noise she made grew louder and higher in pitch.

Young faces peered out inquisitively at the commotion.

"Ma'am, I'm required to inform you that Seaman Santana was killed in the line of duty as he was responding to a terrorist threat yesterday. For his actions the United Nations Peacekeeping Force has posthumously awarded him the Star of Valor." The other man handed over a small velvet box, which contained a gaudy silver medal. On seeing it Maria shrieked even louder and beat her fists weakly on the doorframe. The hesitation between the visitors was obvious, and in the end one of them sighed and reached into a pocket to draw out a pamphlet.

"Here are some people you may want to call," he said as he held it out to her, eventually just setting it down beside where she sat. "Once again on behalf of our commander in chief and the UNPF, you have our deepest sympathies."

With that, they walked away, hearing the crying ramp up another notch as the sobbing of children was added to its cacophony. The two men reached the transport and removed their hats as they stepped stiffly inside.

Once cocooned safely inside the sub-atmospheric ship, the two men relaxed.

"Jesus, Phil," the driver said, "why do they always cry like that? I mean it's not like they don't know this could happen any day, right?"

"I dunno, man," the other said. "You ask me, this has to be the shittiest assignment I ever had. Where's the next one?"

"One in Utah," Phil answered from memory, "one in Pittsburgh. Rock, paper, scissors for driving the longest leg?"

As one, they raised their fists near to one another, bounced them in the air three times and opened them in gestures that they held still. Phil's flat palm was chopped by his partner's fingers that mimicked a pair of scissors.

"Aw, shit," Phil answered, hitting a button for the flight controls to retract into the dash as his partner sat up to meet the instruments that rose in front of him. "How long until Utah?"

"About thirty-five minutes," he answered. "Better get your rest because you're upsetting the next grieving widow or mother."

The UNPF transport took off, rising vertically until it turned its nose to point east, then with a whistling hum of engines, it accelerated away.

CHAPTER 6

CTSF Training Area, Xinjiang, China

Six Years Later

"Grip, this is Bulldog."

"Grip," Commander Leslie Brandt said into the radio in her clipped tones.

"Principal approaching," the very British voice of her second in command said. "Vehicle stopping in four, three, two…"

"Phoenix and Tower, confirm you have eyes on," Brandt said.

"Phoenix," came the bodiless reply in her ear as she watched the five separate screens displayed on the holoprojector before her.

"Got eyeball," the Canadian soldier responded.

Brandt saw him on screen as he approached the vehicle from the right. She swore he glanced directly at the surveillance drone as he did so. His callsign, Tower, was as sarcastic as the rest of him. Standing at five-feet-six in his boots, the man suffered endless teasing about his height, so he had pretended to love the callsign given to him as a joke at the jokers.

Brandt let the radio discipline slide as he was ruthlessly effective, but she reminded herself to add it to the debrief.

"Tower, hold principal until all callsigns report clear. Acknowledge," Brandt said.

"Acknowledged."

"Bulldog, clear."

"Phoenix, clear."

"All units from Grip... *go*."

Tower opened the car door, ushering the principal out as the direct feeds from Bulldog and Phoenix showed systematic scanning around the area of the principal heading up the stairs to the building with Tower covering him with his body. The window of exposure was small, but it was enough.

A bright red blossom appeared on the back of Tower's left arm just above the elbow, and directly in line with where the principal's neck was.

The radio crackled before a new voice came on.

"All callsigns, stand down, stand down. End of exercise," came the call over the radio from the bored-sounding training staff. "Form on me for debrief."

Brandt snatched off the headset and stopped herself before she threw it down in frustrated temper. Instead, she carefully placed it on the desk, rising and leaving the tiny command post to step out into bright sunlight at the head of the steps where Tower was almost spinning around to try and see the red paint on the back of his arm. Two other people jogged over, their carbines held low, and Brandt locked eyes with Bulldog as both of them wore expressions showing disappointment at their failure.

"How in the *hell*," said the training chief, "did you not see this jackoff?" He pointed behind them to the last person to jog over in the small scenario area. They all looked up to see the smiling face of the last member of their team, the aptly named Zero, walking up with his carbine in his hands. He stopped short, mag-locked the gun to his back over his right shoulder, and grinned.

"That's a good question, Chief. How did you miss me, Commander?"

Brandt said nothing, but simply pulled the pistol from her right thigh and fired a single round at Zero's chest plate. The paint round popped, splashing the smelly dye up into his face and making him blow a raspberry to get the taste off his tongue.

"I didn't miss you, see?" she said.

"You asked for that, Zero. Don't say 'missed'."

"Good point," he said, wiping his chin and looking at the pink tinge on his fingers.

"I don't understand why the drones didn't pick him up," Bulldog said.

He was so-named as he was the only Brit to have reached the stage where they allowed callsigns. The original selection process had started with fifty candidates, sifted and selected from all four territories. They were numbered off and treated the same regardless of the rank they arrived with. When they got down to the final twelve candidates, each were given a callsign depending on something they had done or on their particular skills.

Zero, as imaginatively named as Bulldog and Tower, was by far the best shot of the entire course.

"He was masking it," Phoenix said. She had earned her name by having been almost cut from the program five times. Each time when her back was to the wall she somehow pulled out an exemplary performance to rise from the ashes once more. If these five made it through the final exercises, then they would be deployed as one of the few combined territory close protection teams.

"That's right," said the training chief. "How?"

"Field emitters," Brandt said, "and I didn't scan for the right spectrum of electromagnetic fields."

"Correct."

"Sorry, people," Brandt said. "My bad."

"My bad?" the only man not wearing uniform asked, his Chinese accent making him sound somehow even more annoyed. "A live round would have taken my head off and all you can say is *my bad?*"

Brandt shrugged at the other member of training staff, as if to say that it could have been worse.

"What else? Anyone?" the aggrieved former principal of the scenario asked.

"Comm discipline," Brandt said, shooting a brief but sour glance at Tower.

"What of it?" he asked defensively. The two training staff looked at her for her explanation of why she felt it was important.

"If this was real, and if we had lost a principal, our performance would have been picked apart at an inquiry. Your poor comm discipline," she looked directly down at Tower, "would give a prosecutor an opening to attack our professionalism."

"Valid point. I've seen it happen over simple shit like a high-five being caught on CCTV after a clean terrorist kill, or one of your team pounding a fist after using force to detain a subject. Human rights lawyers will dance all over that like they could almost smell the fresh paint in the condo they were gonna buy after the case. Run it again," the training chief said.

"This time try not to screw up."

~

They didn't screw up, and their official designation as a team came in the typically long-winded format of UNPF-CT-CPT-Sigma Two.

Instead of calling themselves the United Nations Peacekeeping Force Combined Territories Close Protection Team, they were referred to simply as Sigma Two and were one of nearly fifty teams spread out over the territories. Close protection was their official designation, but in truth they were now Special Operations forces trained for any number of different scenarios and almost all of them were counter-terrorist in nature. Their training drills, thought-based exercises as often as physical ones, ranged to cover everything from a mass-casualty/victim-operated explosive device to the quiet interception and assassination of lone-wolf gunmen.

Brandt was awarded command of the team, and only when they had completed their training and been rewarded with the silver shield emblem to wear on the collar of their uniforms, did real names and ranks come out. Before that point, discussing them or attempting to use rank on the course was grounds for getting RTU'd and returned to their original units.

Although they were officially a CT squad, a team from multiple territories, only Bulldog and Phoenix had come from outside the American territory. Phoenix was from North Korea but had been one of the hundreds of UN troops to be exchanged among the territories for continuation and specialism training with a view to standardize globally.

It surprised Brandt to find out that she was one of only two officers on the entire course intake, the other being the British lieutenant. This prompted her to reassess some of her assumptions about leadership and ability. None of the others had risen above master petty officer, but then again, without her unexpected admission into

OTA on a fast-track promotion program she doubted she would have risen any higher.

At that end of the NCO rank spectrum, the men and women were generally there for life, and a chief's job was a matter of filling dead men's shoes.

Since the global conflicts on Earth had ended almost three hundred years ago, there wasn't much opportunity for battlefield promotion, even given the heightened risk of terrorist activity.

The team's orders came, and they were housed at a base in Turkey, at one of the eight strategic locations ready for global deployment; theirs was one of the busiest since it was at the border of three territories.

The base was underground, mainly due to the daily temperatures that reached over a hundred degrees. Their daily regime was mostly conducted under artificial light. Brandt, always wanting to be seen to be thinking outside the box, requisitioned a grav emitter usually installed in the small planetary transports. She got the requisition approved, and got Tower to rig it up to the power supply.

She trained them at Earth-plus-ten percent gravity, forcing their bodies to work harder and develop faster with the exercise. Some of the team thought this pointless, seeing as they were all equipped with the latest generation of powered polymer-rendered armor, but she didn't want them totally reliant on their tech to be the best.

"What if something kicks off and we aren't suited up?" she had asked when her training regime was questioned. "You fit enough to take on someone with just your bare hands?"

The suits were much the same as the old ones. The new formula for melding the carbon Kevlar and titanium polymer made for slightly thinner plates capable of stopping a 12mm round, though the impact could still cause a lot of damage. Instead of the new software patch they were expecting, the team was fitted for whole new armor. Their movement and flexibility were improved slightly, and the inclusion of a 'step-in step-out' feature was a godsend. It meant no more complex suiting-up procedures; the suits opened up for them to literally back in to. The new software, however, was by far superior to the last incarnation and included something called intuitive gesture interaction.

Brandt had ordered a training run outside at midday to test the new armor, and to speed up the integration process. The suit needed movement to adapt to the user effectively. But her ulterior motive was that she expected them to fail her field test, and then she could refuse to accept it. She could then keep their existing armor, which was tried and trusted. They stepped outside, their visors instantly turning mirrored as soon as the oppressive sun hit their faces, and they waited for the suits to heat up their bodies from the cool, air-conditioned subterranean base to the scorching surface of the arid landscape they were in. To their surprise, their HUDs flashed up with the sudden temperature change almost immediately and adjusted the internal suit temperature to keep them cool.

Brandt chalked up the score: suit one, her cynicism nil.

"Two miles," she told her team. "My pace." She set off, doing the curious run that took them years to get fully acclimatized to.

They bounded along at almost forty-five miles per hour; each long, lateral leap carried them a normal person's ten paces, as their servo-driven legs applied superhuman-strength to their limbs. The armor wasn't capable of moving each leg quickly enough to sprint, but the adaptation of movement was an easy pay-off for the ability to move nearly twice as fast as they could without it, and for far longer than they could sustain with their bodies alone.

That said, simply wearing the armor didn't make them fit and strong; It required the physical ability of the user. The initial movement to start the servos firing their limbs explosively took effort.

The score was soon at two points in favor of the suits, when they had covered the first mile in three laps of their complex over a minute faster than they had set previously. The new armor was lighter and easier to use, even though it didn't appear to be much smaller than they had been wearing before. The suits moved faster, reacted quicker and most importantly, had kept them cooler.

Brandt called a stop near the entrance to their facility just before the two-mile mark. She stood still, her chest plate rising and falling in response to her deep breathing.

"Battery check," she said in between breaths.

"Ninety-nine percent," Bulldog said crisply. "We certainly have come a long way since those first exoskeleton suits in the twenty-first century."

"Same," Zero said.

"Still at one hundred," Phoenix answered as they turned to look at the last member of the team.

"Ninety... eight..." Tower said, more out of breath than the others. Their mirrored visors took in each other's faces pointlessly as they only saw their reflections, then Brandt raised her left forearm and tapped at the toughened screen built in to it.

The new tech upgrade made her eyes pop as it interacted with her HUD to project the information ahead of her.

"Whoa," she said. "Guys, check this out."

They followed her lead, tapping on their forearm interfaces until the air immediately in front of them erupted in light. The interactive menu was displayed ahead of them in a kind of virtual reality interface. To anyone not wearing a suit with this new tech, it would look as though they were all trying to do some kind of bad Tai Chi routine all at different times, or maybe they were trying to shoo away the world's slowest wasp, but with the visors activated they could see the options laid out for them.

"Try using the blink feature instead of touching it," Zero said, his own hands now down by his side as he scrolled through the options using his eyes alone.

"Ha!" Bulldog blurted out, giving a snorting bray of a laugh. "Warning: Do not attempt to use this interface when in combat. Failure to pay full attention to your environment could result in serious injury or death. The user assumes full responsibility and risk when using this interface option."

"The hell are you reading, Bulldog?" Zero asked him, his hands still down by his sides and his head unnaturally still as though he had been hypnotized.

"The instruction manual, obviously," Bulldog answered. "Seems as though the upgrades are still subject to health and safety regulations."

"Like those old urban legends about people driving fossil fuel vehicles off cliffs because they were following a nav program?" Phoenix asked.

"Something like that," Brandt told her, taking back control of the group. "Tower, what are the usual battery depletions for a two-mile run on the old suits?"

"Anything up to sixteen percent, but in all likelihood higher in these temperatures. Anyone else still perfectly cool?"

They all were, which was a major bonus for them and allowed for daytime operations in extreme heat just as much as it allowed them to function in extreme cold. They were moving toward an intuitive and interfaced exoskeleton rather than a conventional suit of body armor. The design was being varied, according to Tower who stayed abreast of all things technical, to allow for more specialized use for EVAs in space and underwater-based operations on Earth. This current incarnation was the standard combat model, and they had to admit it was an unexpected improvement.

"Everyone fully integrated?" Brand asked the team, checking to see if their software had adapted to their individual movement patterns. The team confirmed, and she had reached one hundred percent integration before the end of the short run. "Okay, everyone back inside to the range."

As they stepped inside the entrance of the facility to ride the elevator down to their subterranean firing range, the comm on Brandt's forearm chirped and flashed.

She tapped the device, flicking the menu up and trying the blink selection feature to answer the incoming call.

The others watched—their visors had gone back to being transparent—but a privacy feature prevented them from seeing or hearing Brandt's incoming message.

"Commander, Glo-Con," the incoming voice from global command network which tasked the CP teams said, "confirm you are on private comm?"

Brandt's eyes flickered to the padlock icon on the top bar of the comm window.

"Confirmed," she said aloud, not explaining that the rest of her team could hear her responses. "Send message."

"CP Lambda One is en-route to your location. You will assume command of both teams and stand by for mission brief. Out."

Brandt killed the display with a wave of her hand and said nothing.

"Well, Commander?" Bulldog asked politely.

"Yeah, the suspense is killing us, Grip," Tower added. "Brush your teeth and get out the good china, kids," she told them. "We got guests comin' over."

CHAPTER 7

Sapporo Mountains, Japan

"Try again," Doctor Hamada said.

His patient flexed the fingers of his hands, still marveling at the sensation he felt in them after so many years of phantom pain from his missing limbs. He shuffled both feet, again trying to get accustomed to the neural feedback of the tiny rise and fall in pressure. He had grown used to the numbness of prosthetic hands and feet.

"*Go.*"

The subject snatched the gun off his left thigh with his dominant hand and raised it as his right hand cupped the base of the pistol grip to offer better stability. His left index finger squeezed off rounds at a rate not humanly possible for them to be properly aimed, but the subsonic 6mm rounds each found their targets with accuracy that indicated years of training.

He had spent years training, but those years had been interspersed with long periods of recovery and therapy after the latest round of surgeries to further enhance his body and integrate new technology.

At first, when he had been brought around from the yearlong coma he had been kept in, the medical team had treated him very carefully. The only people he spoke to were psychologists with experience in limb loss, sight loss, survivor's guilt, post-traumatic stress and a whole raft of other issues applicable to him. He was unique.

Not unique in that he was the only one to have survived those kinds of injuries and the endless operations to repair and rebuild him, but unique in that he was so focused on recovering and improving himself.

He was driving the project as much as Hamada or any of the bioengineering team were.

Once awake, he had spent the first five months blind, which had been a tactical move on Hamada's part on advice from the psych experts. If he couldn't see the damage but was allowed the time to come to terms with their description, then the shock wouldn't be so severe.

In that time he had been fitted with the melded components that allowed the prosthetics to link to him neurologically, and that took longer than the creation of the bespoke limbs themselves.

He wasn't Jake Santana anymore. He couldn't be, they told him. He had to make a conscious decision to leave that person, that identity, behind and embrace his new life as a pioneer. He had accepted that, believing it with every fiber left of his body, and that was how he had adapted so easily to every change they made to him.

Jake was dead, and he had adopted the name Specter in his place.

The ocular prosthetics had taken almost a year to become fully effective, and the constant adjustments and rejections had caused migraines so severe that he had to be sedated numerous times for the pain to subside. It had been the neuro-interface implants that had posed the biggest challenges. The new software they had been forced to innovate had quickly been adapted for commercial means and the program sold to the UN for considerable profit.

The UN research and development labs based all over the world were lightyears behind the discoveries and innovations that Hyper was making. In the last five years alone almost all of the new tech employed by the UN and combined territories forces off-world were traceable directly to the private company.

That didn't mean they got all of their new tech, however.

With the four prosthetic limbs fitted and covered with the rubberized matte-black suit Specter wore, only his eyes gave him away as different. They shone a bright green, like the ancient night vision optics, and when he focused you could see the iris spinning like the zoom lens it was.

When the feed from two binocular ultra-high-definition cameras was successfully routed through his repaired ocular nerves to the microprocessor implanted in his brain and was married up to the speed and dexterity of his new limbs, the end result was what they saw on the training range. That processor, one of five embedded in his repaired and much-improved body, learned and adapted with each movement he made. The scope for his abilities had an upper limit, but they had yet to reach it. They had yet to even come within sight of it.

"Very nice," Hamada said through a grin, "but the smile is a little crooked, don't you think?"

He turned back and the faintest of whirring noises sounded as Specter's eyes zoomed in to take a closer look.

"Hmm," he said, a slightly metallic synthesized edge to his voice after the fiery explosion had scorched his throat.

He lifted the pistol again toward the target and turned to face Hamada. He smiled as he pulled the trigger twice more, lowering the gun to his left thigh where he released the handle for the weapon to lock magnetically against his suit.

Hamada looked back at the target and laughed out loud. The final two shots, so cockily fired with a no-look approach, had evened up the grin on the smiley face of bullet holes drilled into the featureless face of the target.

"Better?" he asked the doctor.

"Yes," Hamada laughed. "Anyway, Specter, I want you to meet Mister Volkov. He is the man responsible for the new pistol."

He looked down at the gun on his thigh then back to the man facing him with the short and neatly groomed beard. The gun's inventor was younger than expected, so Specter thought he must be either extremely talented or well connected.

He had met a lot of important people in recent years—or at least had been paraded for their interest, amusement or investment—but never anyone from, or at least currently in, government service in any of the four territories.

Specter held out his right hand for Volkov to shake, the lightning-fast speed of his movement catching the man off-guard. He was unaccustomed to being around such a surgically enhanced human being.

"A pleasure to finally make your acquaintance," Volkov said in a businesslike tone. He produced an older model of gun, UN's standard issue universal service pistol, and held it in a way that instantly made Specter recognize that he knew how it worked down to the last micron. The way he held it showed he wanted people to know he wasn't going to fire it.

"Now, if I may offer demonstration?"

He turned his head to the side and two assistants scurried over to the destroyed target.

"If I may?" Volkov said, gesturing at the pistol magnetically glued to the thigh of the thick, black suit.

Specter grasped the grip, feeling the weapon come free the moment he held it, and handed it over with the barrel pointing away from them both.

"Thank you. Now observe how there appears to be two magazine wells? One in the grip of the pistol itself and the other here, ahead of the trigger?" Specter had noticed, but he had been told to test fire the weapon and wait for the explanation. "And of course, you are familiar with this?" he asked, offering the USP to him.

Specter took it, and was accosted by the sudden flash of memory with yellow teeth bared in his face as he pulled the trigger over and over with no effect. He brushed the flashback away as quickly as it had come so that nobody noticed his momentary lapse.

"Of course I do," he said as he smiled. "I could field-strip this in my sleep."

"I'm sure you could," Volkov said with a matching smile that seemed anxious. "Now if you would oblige me with three shots into the target once more? Center mass, if you please."

Specter looked back to see that the assistants had put a mannequin against the firing wall and dressed it in the heavy chest plate of the polymer armor of his previous life. He raised the USP, fighting back the threat of more flashbacks by pulling the trigger, and squeezed off three bullets into the dummy. This time he was sure to group together in a neat triangle instead of putting the second two in the same spot as the first.

"Excellent," Volkov said as he carefully produced a small device from his pocket, which he clicked into the port under the barrel of the new weapon. "Again, with this one now if you please."

Specter swapped weapons with him and adjusted his grip to counter the slight weight increase of the gun. He had seen enough weapons demonstrations in his life to know when he had just been handed the magnum. He set his stance wider and gripped the weapon that little bit tighter without crushing the thing in his artificially strong hands. He fired three times adopting the same triangular shot pattern.

No clanging noises came back. No ping and whine of a ricochet filled the air, instead he simply heard a crackle and fizz as the bullets left the gun before the heavy *chink-chink-chink* of the same small caliber bullets drilling neat holes straight through the armor.

Silence filled the shooting gallery as Specter turned the gun in his hand and inspected it again.

"How?" he asked simply.

"The weapon you are holding is not just an upgraded version of the standard pistol used all over the world but is a totally new design." Volkov explained. "However, the addition of this part charges the rounds fired with the singularity energy."

"You managed to create a singularity that small?" Hamada cut in excitedly.

"No, we have harnessed the energy from a singularity to use, or at least someone has," Volkov answered. "I merely specified what housing I needed it in and they did the rest. My design uses that energy to supercharge the bullets, if you understand?"

They did. Specter turned the small, lightweight and well-balanced gun over and over in his hands marveling at the destructive power contained in something so small.

"What about vehicle and ship armor?" he asked.

In response, Volkov nodded to his assistants again, who shuffled toward the end of the range carrying a large square of polymer alloy blast plating that seemed to be taken from one of the UN reinforced troop transports.

"It is belly plate," Volkov said with a wry smile, "before you ask." They both knew the belly was where the armor was thickest. "Group your shots, if you please."

Specter smiled, raised the gun and drilled a dozen shots into a single spot where the original bullet hole widened with each successive projectile going into the same place. He stopped, lowering the gun and zooming in with his green eyes to see the damage.

"It's penetrated," he said, "just not all the way through."

"With armor this thick there are two ways to approach: more bullets or bigger bullets."

"What have you got?"

"Both," Volkov smiled as wolfishly as his name suggested, snapping his fingers for two small crates to be carried forward.

"So what is to stop our own troops being vulnerable to this new technology?" a technician asked after the impressive display had ended. He earned himself an annoyed look from his superiors at addressing their guest directly. That look lingered until Specter agreed that it was a good question.

"Simply that we are the only ones to possess it," Volkov answered, "and we have another ace up our sleeve, as you say."

"Which is?"

"Shielding."

Specter frowned. "But the smallest we've been able to create a shield is still big enough to need an entire shuttle to carry it. Most vehicles still rely on heavy plate armor because they can't be shielded unless by an emitter array. Now you're going to tell me you've cracked that too?"

"Again, not us," Volkov said, "but another research laboratory. You know how the company likes to keep its assets separated. This is not my gift to give, but I hope you enjoy the new prototypes."

Volkov and his entourage left, no doubt being flown down to Tokyo to be shown a good time by the corporate fixers whose only job was to keep the talent happy and faithful. Specter stayed on the range level alone for a while, no longer requiring a chaperone everywhere he went, if he didn't leave the complex. If the new pistol was an angular and sleek thing of beauty, then the sub-machine gun and the battle rifle he had been left with were in a new league entirely.

Slightly smaller than the same short-barreled bullpup carbine he had been accustomed to, the new prototype was lighter and smaller and yet more balanced and stable than the old version. It was built on a different platform, just as the pistol was totally new and not just an improvement to the existing article. It sported a long, curved magazine that ran under the gun from where it clicked into the stock behind the trigger grip right underneath, to where the molded end of it became part of the foregrip.

Ahead of that, just as with the pistol, the small singularity pod sat smoothly in the housing under the barrel to add that extra kick to the tiny 6mm bullets leaving the muzzle at both sub and supersonic speeds. All it took was the flick of a selector switch.

It had interchangeable ejection ports and short charging handles on each side, so as to be truly ambidextrous in a couple of seconds. This feature was useful to Specter; despite his loss of limbs, his brain had retained the knowledge that he was left-handed. He was equally accurate with his right and could even engage two separate targets using an eye for each, but that left him with headaches and the occasional nosebleed if he did it for too long. In contrast with the underpowered, fiddly and unbalanced Universal Service Rifle, he was holding a masterpiece.

The longer rifle fired the heavier 12mm round usually reserved for the squad support weapons. Heavy caliber guns had been a big thing in the distant past, he knew, but advances in other fields had reduced their need to carry bigger sticks than one another; they just needed better and faster sticks. Following a similar but longer design to the small carbine, he traced his black-tipped fingers over the stenciled legend on the side. HYPR prototype battle rifle 12.

Given the sheer power of these new weapons in comparison with what they could bring down, like governments and spacecraft, he couldn't help feeling that humanity was on the precipice of war once again.

CHAPTER 8

CP Deployment Base, Near Havza, Turkey

"Welcome to our house, Lamba One," Tower said ebulliently as he greeted the looming man in helmetless armor at the head of the five-man team.

"Who are you?" an unexpectedly harsh and familiar voice answered. Brandt recognized the accent and tone instantly, and it threatened to take her back to a time when she only followed orders and didn't give them.

"Tower," Tower, said smiling.

"Well, stand up when you are talking to me," Chief said. Laughter rippled around all ten of them, the loudest coming from Tower's own teammates.

"Chief," Brandt said as she stood to look up into the rich brown eyes of her former top NCO. She was a tall woman, but she still had to crane her neck a little.

"You are Commander Brandt," Chief said, a statement and not a question. Brandt saw the look in his eyes and knew that he recognized her. She didn't like the hostility she saw either.

"Chief," she said in a low voice, "care to talk in private?" He nodded his assent and she led the way to her office. She shut the door on the windowless environment and sat on the edge of her desk to face the hulking man in full battle armor with a sidearm holstered on the front of his right thigh.

"Have you seen the mission brief yet?" he asked.

"No, Glo-Con said you would be bringing it in person for security reasons." His eyes narrowed slightly, and his mouth drew tighter.

He pulled out an old-fashioned data disk, a small hexagonal piece of light blue polymer with a web of gold lines embedded in the plastic. He didn't ask or wait for an invitation, merely spun her terminal around and stuck the disk into the feed on the side of the screen. The black screen blinked, then a scrolling line of text came up. Brandt stooped to read as it went, filling the screen before stepping upward incrementally. Her eyes flickered left and right as she read until the screen ticked up to show a face in both front and side aspects. The picture was an enhanced image cut from surveillance footage and wasn't a standard identification photo or a mugshot.

Chief evidently couldn't wait for the intelligence report to finish and started speaking.

"This man, this Oscar Wilkins, he is to make an attempt on the African Territory's president tomorrow."

"Alone?" she asked, wondering how one person could be so delusional as to think that they could tangle with the UN on their own.

"He is part of a wider conspiracy, but from what the Intelligence Directorate believes, he has only moral and technical support; no boots on the ground."

"How have they gotten this?" she asked. He smirked, offering a slight shrug of his shoulders in response. *Who knows how the UNID operate?* it said.

"Method?" she asked.

"Lone gunman or victim-worn explosive device," Chief told her. "VWED, nasty."

"Your team is up to date on the latest tactics?"

"Please, Chief," she said wearily. "We may be new to CP but not fresh outta basic."

He wasn't moved and stared at her until she answered the question.

"Head shot, brainstem destruction to prevent activation and deployment of electronic countermeasures in case of biometric failsafes or a DMS."

The chief nodded his satisfaction, his brow wrinkling slightly as he remembered how much he hated a dead man's switch device.

They discussed the method and picked apart the intelligence they had, deciding the best way to go about the mission. When the chief offered an alternative opinion to Brandt's suggestion they found themselves obligated to address the elephant in the room.

"I appreciate that, Chief," Brandt said, "but with all d..." she stopped herself, recalling his words the last time she tried to placate him with her due respect. He recognized the moment for what it was, but instead of smiling and making it easy for her, he kept his mouth in a grim straight line and cocked a single eyebrow.

"This is my mission, Chief. Glo-Con put me in charge, which I'm sure you know." She locked eyes with him, waiting for the tension to either fade or break. It didn't, and she sighed as she had to lay it out.

"Listen, Chief," she started before frowning and asking a question. "Hey, what's your CP callsign?"

"Chief," the chief said.

Imaginative, Brandt thought, then reinforced the name she had been given and got a grip of herself.

"Listen, Chief, I guess you don't like it but you're going to have to suck it up and deal with it." Something inside her quivered with palpable fear as she addressed the man she had lived in actual fear of for years.

Despite the six years and her very recent elevation to the rank of commander, it was clear that he still saw her as a jumped-up grunt with no business commanding troops, and most specifically no business commanding *him*. She steeled herself, the anger at the constant assumption that just because she was a track, and more specifically because she was a female track, she hadn't dedicated her life to being a professional soldier. She trained, learned, studied and in some way prepared for a new scenario to land on her head every single day.

Her life was the UNPF, and she knew she was capable of so much more, even if she had cheated through official channels to get there. Her acceptance into the CP training program was the final favor owed to her from the fast-track course, but passing that course and everything from there on out that she achieved would be on merit alone. She didn't want that to be some god-awful guard detail or rural peacekeeping command at the ass-end of nowhere, so she chose special operations to make her mark.

"As I said, we will intercept him en-route and take him down quietly," she told the chief who now wore a veiled look of mild amusement. "The city will be crawling with armor anyway, so in full rigs we won't look out of place. My team will do the takedown and yours will provide cover, got that?"

The chief looked at her, one blood vessel in his left temple pulsating and setting her imagination off down a wild rabbit hole. The pulsating grew more rapid and seemed like it could burst at any second.

"I understand my orders, *Commander,*" he said, a hint of ice in his words but nothing anywhere near as malicious as she remembered him to be. *Perhaps SpecOps has chilled him out?*

"What if your primary method fails?" he asked her eventually.

She stopped, thinking of the options and giving the answer in a second.

"Then we double down on the principal, inform him of the threat and treat it like a straight-up CP job with an outer-cordon team in place to take the subject."

The chief nodded, no sign of agreement or dispute on his face. He was infuriatingly neutral.

"Why are you here?" he asked, shocking her with the subject change. "Still in the UNPF I mean? Weren't you offered a discharge?"

Brandt thought back to the day she had read her orders aloud to Paterson and the wheel, leaving out the option to take a compensation payout and honorable discharge for the injuries she'd received in the line of duty. She had dismissed the thought out of hand, even declining to attend a medal ceremony and having her Purple Wreath sent to her by courier. It sat in her quarters at the officer training academy unopened. In fact, it was still unopened, but the assistant from the adjutant's corps had attached the ribbon to her dress uniform. She had worn that uniform for promotion ceremonies, but the small wreath medal awarded to celebrate her being shot and rendered useless didn't make her feel any sense of pride. If she hadn't been unconscious and bleeding, if she hadn't been incapacitated which led to the medal, then Jake might still be alive.

She fixed the chief, her former boss, with a look that conveyed he was overstepping. Instead of apologizing or backing off he just stared at her, waiting for the answer. She relented, tapping at her datapad and spinning it around on the table for him to see.

The image of three young soldiers looked back at him. The swarthy and good-looking Latino features of Jake Santana grinned beside her face, which was somehow much younger than the six years that had passed would dictate. It was as though her innocence still existed back when the image was captured and now her dedication to the UNPF had aged her soul as well as her body. On the other side of her smiling face was Jamie Paterson, ducking down so that his annoying and ungainly height put him at the same level as their faces. He was making a stupid face, no doubt intended to annoy Brandt. He had always goaded her like a kid in school trying to be mean to the girl he liked because he lacked the vocabulary to express his feelings. Chief knew that was crap because Paterson, despite being too tall for his own good, was one of the sharpest minds in the entire unit back then and that included the officers. He remembered something about Paterson only being there to earn his way into college and that had been his payout for keeping his mouth shut about what had happened to them on the Moon.

"That's why I'm here," she told him. "Because he's dead and I couldn't stop it. I have a debt to pay, and I serve for both of us."

"That is a load of bullshit," the chief said. "You serve for yourself, regardless of these motivations you claim. We should brief our teams and get ready to move out."

Cape Town, South Africa

"Bulldog, Grip," Brandt said from the small, windowless room she occupied.

The new armor software removed the need to have hardwired screens; her hands waved over the interface and brought up the various closed-circuit loops and the constantly searching facial recognition program.

"Bulldog receiving," his crisp and polite voice came back.

78

"Still nothing on facial-rec. Prepare to fall back to secondary positions and take control of principal." She was nervous, sweating inside her armor and seeing the small icon flash in the lower corner of her HUD to indicate that the internal temperature was lowering to adapt to the change. She put it from her mind and concentrated on what she could directly affect.

Bulldog acknowledged the order and left his position, moving to the government offices two blocks away from the train station they were watching. Per their intel, they expected the subject would approach the target area by rail. Brandt ran her fingers through the air, the gestures accessing the communications channels and opening up a private comm between her and the chief.

"Chief, you get my last?" she muttered as her eyes continued scanning the four screens floating in front of her.

"I heard you," he said sounding annoyed, "and I told you this would happen."

He hadn't, not specifically, and Brandt bit her lip not to respond.

"Irrelevant," she snapped. "Stay fluid and get a grip of what we have in front of us."

The chief said nothing before she'd cut off their comm link. She only made the channel private to save face in case he was negative about their results for the other eight CP troops to hear.

She was worried. Worried because she'd envisaged intercepting the subject as he exited the train station, diverting him quietly out of the crowd and slapping an electronic countermeasure device on him to prevent any kind of signal from detonating what he carried, if he even carried anything. Their drones were still sitting on the roof of the tallest building on the block near to the government offices; their presence could be explained by a simple communique to the African territory headquarters security division of the UNPF to announce their presence in the area of operations. Such notifications were commonplace, and any UNPF soldier aware of the presence of a CP team would know nothing more unless they were needed.

"Okay, all callsigns prepare to move in five. Stay on station."

~

Bulldog strode straight into the main government office building, his new model armor with its steel-gray paint and the lack of rank speaking volumes without him saying a word. As his only badge of authority, his armor bore the shield emblem of the CP teams on the front of his right shoulder and the symbol of his team designation, the angular backward three of sigma, on the side of his right arm as well as on the rear of his helmet.

"Your officer in charge, please," he ordered politely, watching as the woman looked up at him, widened her eyes and stuttered as she reached for the phone. Her shock made her move with less efficiency than Bulldog liked. "If we could hurry it along?"

Within two minutes, he was addressing the lieutenant commander in charge of the government building security detail.

"Where is your commander?" Bulldog's voice came over the speaker of his suit. He had intentionally not removed his helmet, though it was their protocol when dealing with standard units on deployment.

"He, er…" the officer stammered as he tried to gauge the seniority of the man before him. "He sent me in his place."

This was part of the reason the armor bore no rank and kept their faces covered. Then the people they dealt with had to deal with the reputation of special operations instead of an individual. The standing order for every UN troop when dealing with any member of the CP teams was to offer them any and all assistance as directed.

Bulldog mocked the man, feigning a comedic attempt at his accent. "He sent you in his place, did he? Well, did he even bother to ask why I was here?" The man had no answer, and Bulldog's annoyed sigh came through the speakers a little too obviously. "I want every available soldier on external cordon," he ordered with a sudden additional gravity to his voice. "Your people around the president will continue to do as they would, only I will be taking direct control of the detail. They will do exactly what I tell them to, when I tell them to do it. With me so far?"

The officer nodded.

"Our teams are not to be distracted, molested or in any way hindered. We have a credible threat to life and we will deal with it."

The young man nodded again, assimilating all of this unexpected information and trying to prioritize his response. Any response was too slow in coming for Bulldog, who hurried him along.

"Well, move your bloody arse, you buffoon! Go and get your commander and tell him everything I told you. Go!" The officer scampered away, almost knocking down the two junior aides who fled in his wake. Inside his mirrored visor Bulldog smiled to himself, suspecting that he was probably going to hell one day but happy that at least he'd be warm when he got there.

~

"Okay, all callsigns, I will maintain electronic overwatch," Brandt said inside her helmet. She had gestured over the projection of the group channel icon to transmit on open mic. "Fall back and concentrate on final positions to cover the principal at target window. Acknowledge."

One by one they called in their callsign to acknowledge their orders as Brandt watched their position markers on her HUD blink. She kept her eyes flickering between the constantly scanning facial recognition software linked to the closed-circuit channels at the train station. She expanded that to link to the citywide network, almost physically feeling the additional drain on the server she had connected to while running the active search.

Nothing. No sign of the subject at all. The facial recognition search protocols automatically flagged anyone with facial coverings as they had been outlawed generations before, but even the anomalous reads were all wrong. If she had to guess, which she didn't like doing, he wasn't there. As the time ticked down to the president's departure, she grew more and more nervous and her suit reacted again to lower the temperature and draw the moisture out of the internal atmosphere into the recycler.

"Arrival in six minutes," Bulldog announced over the channel, having taken over control of the team set to escort the president out of the offices. "Confirm no sighting of subject?"

"Negative," she answered. "No sighting of subject. Alternative exits by motorcade?"

"No internal parking," Bulldog reported. "Street side or nothing."

"No alternative exits?"

"Side street, too open," he reported.

Brandt chewed her lip, her eyes flickering over the displays like she was plugged in directly to the system.

"Recommend we abort and withdraw," the chief's voice

grumbled over the comm. He had said it on the open channel, which angered Brandt; he should have extended the courtesy of using a private link between them and now she faced a disagreement in front of both teams.

"Negative, maintain positions and respond to any incident."

"Grip, this is Bulldog. Principal standing by to exit. Go or no go, over?"

"Commander," the chief said cutting in before she could respond, "with all due respect, I recommend we abort."

Silence hung on the channel as all the members of their respective teams waited to see how it would play out.

"Negative," Brandt snapped a little more unprofessionally than she liked. "Stay on station. Bulldog, you are a go."

"Understood, moving now."

Two things happened simultaneously.

The facial recognition program flashed red borders around a live feed and brought up the file images of the subject.

As she reached for it to drag it to the center of her holo-display and identify where that camera was, she called a standby over the radio, just as she registered the figures in the background behind the captured image. Those of her second-in-command and the president.

Bulldog put his armored left arm over the shoulder of the principal as he sent the man's own team out of the main exit ahead of them, just as two more sigma team members flanked them. As her eyes flickered back to their subject, the screen blossomed a bright orange and a concussive rumble shook the ground beneath her. The sound of the explosion was deafening to anyone at street level as glass and steel and atomized body parts blew outwards from the ground floor of the government offices.

Brandt stood transfixed, her eyes just watching the building burn.

"Bulldog, Grip," she tried weakly. No response.

"Phoenix, Grip." No response.

"Tower, Grip." Nothing.

"All callsigns," she said in a trance, realizing that she didn't know what to say next.

"All callsigns..."

"All callsigns, this is Chief. Move in and secure attack site. Primary task is recovery of injured personnel. EMTs and additional UNPF troops are on their way. Move." A pause. "Commander, stand down. I repeat, stand down."

~

In the chaos surrounding the explosion, a shrouded male figure stopped and removed the oversized poncho he wore to reveal the local uniform of a firefighter.

He slipped inside the tall building via the fire escape doors, which burst open as those unaffected by the blast from the fourth floor upward came out like a tidal wave. He ushered those people to safety, giving clear instructions like a firefighter would in such a situation. Nobody thought to question why he was there alone, or why he didn't carry any equipment or where the engine he belonged to was. Nobody noticed the electronic twang to his voice because it simply wasn't relevant to them after a bomb had just gone off. People saw what their minds allowed them to see, and in the wake of a terrorist bombing at their building, these people just wanted safety and sunlight that wasn't obscured by the roiling black clouds of smoke as the front lower floors of the office block burned.

When the flow of bodies subsided, the figure began to climb the stairs. He met others in ones and twos, directing them down to street level with confident commands as he climbed quickly, abnormally quickly in fact. Despite his almost-vertical sprint he wasn't sweating and was barely breathing heavily by the time he reached the eighth floor. He pushed open the double doors that bore no sign to indicate what had happened on the other side. He ignored the biometric security lock, which, along with the security cameras, had been instantly disabled as soon as the building's systems had detected the blast.

The man strode through the lab, seeming to know where he was heading but also giving off the impression that he was working to a detailed description and not personal knowledge. He went through three other doors, reaching a section of the floor only accessible through the heavy door, which looked like the front of an old-fashioned bank vault.

It was analogue and stand-alone, with no connectivity to any external server or system to prevent it being hacked. The simple location of the vault, eight floors up in the UN government building, had been deemed sufficient to keep it safe. But it wasn't.

"Code?" he said softly, waiting for a response that was unheard by anyone else and nodded. The man spun the dial on the vault door left, then right, then left again twice more before the door opened with a slight atmospheric pop of escaping gases.

Again, he appeared to know precisely where to look as he discounted the obvious wealth of rhodium, platinum and gold ingots. Instead he pulled a small stack of datapads from one specific box, before stuffing them into custom-made pockets inside the coat of his fake uniform.

Silently, he closed the door, spun the dial to lock it once more, and retraced his steps rapidly to ground level. There he disappeared into the crowds.

CHAPTER 9

UNPF Headquarters, Roosevelt Island

Brandt had wanted to walk to her court martial hearing, but the two UNPF MPs with their white armbands insisted that she be brought to headquarters under escort. She had wanted to stroll past the ancient ruins of the old headquarters building on the banks of the East River, where they were preserved as a monument to the global war that had consumed every continent on Earth. Somehow the twisted metal beams and green hillocks of crumbled concrete calmed her; they reminded her that everything had moved on that time when her entire race was hell-bent on tearing itself apart. The walk would have taken her an hour, or longer since she knew she wouldn't have resisted stopping to eat something at one of the food outlets along the way. She wanted to wander over the pedestrian section of the Marley Bridge, named after one of the pioneers of lunar habitation and the creator of the gravity emitters they relied on so heavily. She wanted to run her hands over the old plaque that explained how the bridge had been rebuilt and renamed almost fifty years after the war when it had been hit by an aerial bombardment by the British. It had been the Queensborough Bridge back then, and even the name brought to mind the ancient colonial ways of her country's lineage.

She had enjoyed Manhattan just as she always did. Her rank allowed her to use the hotels in the city instead of being confined to barracks during curfew like the enlisted soldiers. The other benefit of her rank was that she was permitted to stay there and report in remotely twice each day under the guise of being on 'technical leave' instead of being held under guard at the nearest barracks.

Instead of walking, instead of sampling the culinary delights and risking getting some kind of hot sauce down the front of her white uniform, and instead of feeling somehow connected to history through the physical contact, she found herself under guard sitting in the back of the dull government transport ship hopping over the gray water of the river below, and depositing them inside the gray compound walls of the UN. She stepped out, squinting at the sunlight, which seemed to belie the chill fall temperature.

"Commander Leslie Brandt?" called a young officer wearing the stars of a lieutenant on his right shoulder.

"Yes."

"Lieutenant Andrew Nance, UN Attorney's staff," he said, introducing himself. He seemed flustered and young for a lieutenant. Brandt smiled and said none of these observations out loud. She didn't want him any more stressed than he already seemed.

"So how are we looking?" she asked as she walked, waiting for him to scurry alongside her and catch up.

"We, er," he said. "We have a number of options for your defense strategy."

"Which are?" Brandt said as she walked through the scanner at security. The UN guard stared at the screen as though he were playing a video game. He didn't once look up to connect with the very real person he was seeing displayed in different colors through the image scanner.

"Well, you—*we*—could plead that the UN put you into a position of command ahead of your experi—"

"No," Brandt cut him off. "Next." She stopped at the coffee machine and tapped the screen for her selection of black with extra sugar before holding her right thumb on the reader for payment. A paper cup dropped down as the machine whirred to life.

"Three credits for a coffee?" she mused aloud. "I bet it's shit, too."

"I've listened to the radio transmission recording," Nance tried. "We could imply that the interference of the other team leader was detrimental to the command and control of the mission. Command Chief On... Onyi... Onyilog... Lambda One's commander," he said, giving up on the pronunciation.

"No," Brandt said. "Blaming the chief is *not* the way to approach this."

"Okay, so we go after the source of the intelligence," Nance said. "How were you to know that the terrorist was already there and had access to the government buildings? How were you to know that he had somehow disabled the explosive material detectors in the lobby?"

"You want to go after the Intelligence Directorate?" Brandt asked him with incredulity. "Lieutenant, are you just young and inexperienced or do you have an ambition to find yourself on external foot patrol duties on the lunar surface?"

"Well, I can only suggest that you fall on your sword," Nance said, sounding a little hurt and annoyed but trying to remain professional, "because if you aren't willing to divert the blame away from yourself then there is little I can do to help you."

"The responsibility *is* mine," she said to him, "and that is what I'll tell the court martial."

Nance fixed her with a look and muttered, "Your funeral."

Brandt said nothing. She sat on a bench and leaned back carefully so as not to crease her uniform. She sipped the coffee. It wasn't that bad, which surprised her, but it still wasn't worth a full three credits. She looked around for any other source of hot, wet caffeine and smiled grimly as she found none.

You can charge what you like when you're the only show in town.

She refused to blame anyone else for what happened. She had known as soon as it went wrong that she should have cancelled the operation, moved the president back inside and played it safe. She had spent a lot of time in the previous weeks going over the events of that day, and that period of reflection was interrupted not by thoughts of her own funeral, but by the three ceremonies she attended for her dead team members. Some of the people there had looked at her with sympathy, knowing that she felt the loss and the guilt keenly, but others were unkind to her. Bulldog's wife, a pretty but sharp-tongued woman who was far younger than Brandt would have expected, wanted the officer to look her in the eye when she explained how her husband had been flash-cooked inside his armor. Her face cracked at this, not because of the pain she saw in another woman's face but for the sting of memory when she had found their intact armor suits. Her own HUD showed zero life signs but what was curious was that data of their suits showed them having a water-recycling malfunction. It was only afterwards that she realized that malfunction was their liquefied insides leaking out of them and instantly clogging up the filters. She had been violently sick then. The imagery only served to magnify the knowledge that she had made the wrong call and that hundreds of people had died.

Why had she insisted on staying the course when she should have withdrawn? Was it arrogance? Pride? Was it sheer stubbornness that she wanted to prove that she was in charge now?

Whatever it had been, whatever her soul-searching had uncovered, it did nothing to change the fact that they were dead for following her orders.

As she allowed herself a brief dip in a shallow pool of self-pity, a figure walking up to security was caught by her peripheral vision. Whoever it was set off a small alarm inside her brain. She didn't turn to look—she had been too well trained for that—but she kept the blurred shape just inside her field of vision as it passed through the checkpoint.

She watched as he glided across the floor, head barely moving from side to side, but certain that he had catalogued everyone and everything in the busy public area. He was wearing a dress uniform that looked brand new, which it probably was. She knew for a fact that the wearer wasn't one for formal occasions and that he wanted to pull at the collar and avoid the glare from the medals on his chest. He walked smoothly toward the same coffee machine she had used. As he did, she watched him from the peripheral vision of her right eye. She leaned back to sip her drink and get a better angle with a natural and unhurried movement. He selected his coffee order, black with one sugar if she knew him at all, which she did, and relaxed as he walked past her to settle himself down on the bench over her left shoulder.

"Well, fancy seeing you here," Zero said in a voice that was only loud enough for her to hear.

Always was a master of the covert stuff, Brandt thought to herself.

"Slow day," Brandt answered. "Thought I'd get my ass kicked out of the corps. I guess that's why you're here?"

"Yup," he said, drawing out the sound. "I'm to testify that you argued with the boss of Lambda team and got distracted yada yadda…"

"You're to testify that I'm to blame," Brandt said flatly. No accusation, just facts.

"No, ma'am," he answered, awarding her the honorific not for her rank but for his upbringing. "I can't say what's not true under oath, now, can I?"

"But I am responsible."

"That's a maybe," Zero answered equably. "Part of the *responsibility* of what went down is on you, because it was your team and you were in charge. We all have to live with shit and I imagine that weighs heavy on your soul, but you aren't to *blame*. Remember that difference, Grip."

She was saved any answer by the impossibly young Lieutenant Nance waving at her from across the lobby.

"Commander Brandt? They're ready for you now."

Brandt stood, smoothed down her dress uniform and left her coffee on the bench as she walked tall to meet her fate, and carry the weight of her responsibility.

~

"All rise," the clerk announced. Brandt stood to attention and waited for the three admirals to enter. As with all other uniformed men and women in the room, she snapped a salute and held it until the two old men and one old woman sat down and removed their headgear. Brandt dropped her arm, waiting to be ordered to sit.

"This court martial has been convened," the admiral in the center seat began without preamble, talking in an almost bored-sounding voice, "to establish the facts pertaining to the terrorist attack in South Africa and the failings, if there are any to be found, of the officer overseeing that mission, Commander Leslie Brandt. Commander?"

Brandt sat up straight and looked him in the eye. "Are you satisfied that you have had sufficient time to discuss your case with counsel, which has been provided to you free of charge by the United Nations Peacekeeping Force?"

"Sir," she replied crisply. "Yes, sir, I am."

"Good, then we shall begin. Commander Morello, are you ready to proceed?"

A tall, good-looking officer stood at the table to her right. His hair had turned the color of titanium, prematurely she had to guess, given his smooth movements and obvious fitness. She found herself admiring the man who was about to prosecute her.

"Sir, if I may?" she said loudly, standing to attention. All eyes turned to her including, she could feel, the interested eyes of the man who had been about to destroy her actions and decisions in his opening statements.

"What is it, Commander?" asked the admiral to the right, his voice rich and accented with something she could only guess as European. *Italian? French? Definitely not Spanish...*

She got a grip of her thoughts and cleared her throat.

"Sir, if it would please this court martial, perhaps I would be permitted to explain something?"

"You'll have your opportunity to refute the charges, Commander," the same admiral said harshly.

"That's just it, sir," she said. "I do not intend to refute the charges. I have been charged with poor decision-making causing the death of ninety-eight civilians, thirty-one UN personnel, three of my teammates and one president. I plead guilty to this charge."

Stunned silence filled the small room.

"My counsel has advised to apportion at least some of the blame elsewhere, but I do not believe this is right. Yes the intelligence was wildly inaccurate on the timing and location of the attack, and yes, there were factors that could be called a distraction, but none of that changed the fact that my orders were carried out and those one hundred and thirty-three people died because of those orders. I accept full responsibility for what happened." She nodded and stood rigid to attention, waiting for permission to sit once again. Morello had remained standing as she spoke, and now cleared his own throat and addressed the admirals.

"If it please this court martial," he said with only a hint of mockery for her words, "the prosecution would seek to accept this admission of responsibility and recommend a lenient punishment. Demotion and transfer off-world would satisfy. I am required to offer the court a copy of a letter of recommendation from the UNID." He stepped forward lithely, holding up his own datapad and waiting for the three admirals to tap at the screens in front of them, before he gestured along his screen to swipe the letter toward them. They read in silence, eyebrows raising as they read.

Brandt stood stock still, not relaxing one inch until she was permitted to. It had become a matter of pride not to crack, not to show weakness or exhaustion, but to wait resolutely as the admirals bent their heads together in conference.

The Intelligence Directorate getting involved? she thought. *Something stinks now, I'm sure of it.*

"Commander Brandt," the lead admiral announced loudly, "for your failure of leadership *indirectly* causing the death of the one hundred and thirty-three people mentioned, you are hereby demoted to the rank of lieutenant commander effective immediately. Your status as CP has been revoked and all the incumbent privileges that go along with both rank and status are now denied to you. You will receive orders when they have been drawn up and you are forfeit one year's pay." He picked up the gavel and tapped it once almost lazily on the wooden top of their raised table before the clerk called for them all to rise once more. The three admirals shuffled out of the room after the shortest court-martial any of them had ever experienced.

Brandt turned to Nance, the younger officer's eyes wide with shock. She patted him on the shoulder.

"Good job," she told him.

"I didn't..." he stammered.

"I know, but a win is a win. Don't look too hard at it." She stepped away from the desk and turned to see the fine features of Commander Morello looking curiously at her. She remembered herself and saluted.

"You've been a junior rank to me for less than half a minute," he said kindly. "You can dispense with the salutes and the Sirs for now."

Brandt dropped her hand and allowed a small smile to cross her face, despite the devastatingly fatal blow her career had just suffered. "Sir, may I see that report?"

"Sadly, no," Morello told her with a mischievous smile of his own. "One of the conditions of the report was that it was not to reach open court and has been destroyed now. No mention of it will be in the official records of the hearing." Brandt looked confused and disappointed.

"What I can permit you to do, however," Morello said, "is join me for dinner later."

Brandt's eyes narrowed, assessing the ground for signs of an ambush.

"So..." she began slowly and suspiciously, "you just prosecuted me and demoted me, had me transferred off-world probably forever and *now* you want to buy me dinner?"

"Hey, I never said I was buying..." he answered with his hands out to his sides.

"Condition of agreement," she told him, "I pick the place and you pick up the check."

"Agreed," he laughed. "Corner of Third and East Forty-Second, right?" He chuckled at her horrified expression. "Relax, I sent the transport to collect you."

She screwed her mouth up a little as she thought. "Eight-thirty."

"I'll pick you up," he agreed.

"No, meet me there at eight-thirty and we'll walk." Morello agreed before turning back to her, wearing an apologetically awkward look. "One more thing..." He reached out and gently unclipped the shield badge from her uniform, reaching into his pocket and coming out with the three-starred emblem of her newly demoted rank.

"Had that one planned in advance, huh?" she asked him.

CHAPTER 10

Lower East Side, NYC

Brandt changed out of her clothes at the headquarters building, cheating the system by requisitioning fresh PT gear from the gym there and bagging her uniform to be cleaned and collected whenever she had need of it again, which she suspected would probably be never. Wearing the gray jogging suit and white sneakers with the UNPF logo on made her feel a little less conspicuous than the crisp, white dress uniform complete with medals.

She was not a native New Yorker, not by a thousand miles, but it was where she based herself whenever she was on extended periods of leave. A couple of times Brandt had travelled to the southwest to visit with Jake or to the Virginia coast with Paterson, but not having any real family home herself— she didn't get along with her mother—she had chosen the oddly comfortable yet seemingly inhospitable city as the place where her soul belonged.

She walked the route back, crossing the bridge and running her fingertips over the plaque before hitting the street feeling almost a little refreshed. She had gone to her court martial with all the dignity she possessed, expecting to be facing a sanction on a sliding scale somewhere between a dishonorable discharge and life imprisonment. Now it was possible she would spend the rest of her service guarding the shower block on night duty on a base with only five people on and being perpetually stuck in a rank where she would never fully be in command ever again.

But at least, she told herself, *she was still in the service.*

With the terror threats escalating daily, it was unlikely that she would be based somewhere that was so safe it would be boring, but she knew that high-profile assignments were never going to come her way again. The best she could hope for would likely be a punishment posting.

She put all of that out of her mind as she walked, taking in the sights and sounds and smells of the city. She had seen old movies depicting the place as a noisy, bustling place. There had been areas where everyone walked in fear of being robbed and others where some of the biggest transfers of wealth took place just blocks away.

She experienced none of that now, and only the thrum of repulser and thruster engines stirred the air above the comings and goings of the people at street level. So much of what went on in the cities happened way above ground level but there was something about the street that made her feel... *connected.* She took her time, wandering back to her hotel and musing about the strange turn of events the day had taken. She checked her watch, calculating the hours she had left before she had to get herself showered and ready to go out. She had time for a nap first.

Who knows? She thought. *It might be a late night.*

Dressed in a simple black top and matching jeans, Brandt stepped out onto the sidewalk and sucked in a lungful of city air through her nose. It wasn't warm, but neither was it cold enough to warrant a jacket. Her clothes were simple, functional, but their tight cut gave heavy hints to her physical attributes.

Dead on eight-thirty, Morello rounded the corner of Third to her left. He wore blue denim jeans under a white shirt and sports coat, blending the casual with the formal effortlessly. He wore it as well as he wore his dress uniform. His collared shirt was unbuttoned perhaps one button too many for her liking but his off-duty look emphasized his air of the charismatic Italian descendant.

Brandt took another breath and put on her winning smile.

"Commander," she greeted him, offering him her hand to shake.

"Anthony, please," he said as he leaned in to lightly kiss both cheeks in turn. Brandt felt her face flush as he did so, disarming her effectively. She fought down the unexpected urge to reply with "*Ayy, Tony*" like in classic gangster movies.

"Leslie," she responded, feeling odd to go by her first name when every day of her life she was addressed either by rank, surname or callsign.

No callsign any more, she thought sourly before shaking it off.

"Leslie," Morello repeated with a smile. "So, where are we going?"

"Just a little place I know nearby," she told him. "Come on."

She set off, jaywalking with impunity across the road in between the sparse traffic of small yellow and black transports. Morello followed, catching up easily within a few strides.

"You from here?" he asked conversationally. Something told her that he already knew she wasn't, but she humored him with an answer anyway.

"No, I just like it here," she told him, leaving out the fact that she had been saving to buy her own place there eventually. "You are though."

"Born and raised. Grew up on Canal with a brother and a sister. Mother was in the service and father was a lawyer."

Brandt frowned internally at that, unsure why she felt the traditional role reversal was an issue. "Went to join straight after high school and got diverted into the UN Attorney's staff. Did my law degree and been there ever since. Thirteen years now."

"And there was me expecting some 'son of the admiral' story..."

"Hardly, not me anyway," he laughed cryptically.

They walked in silence for a while, separating to dodge the oncoming pedestrians who threatened to break-up any conversation they struck up. They both moved like native city-dwellers: dodging and overtaking with ease as they gauged the speed of the oncoming human traffic. Brandt stopped by the edge of the sidewalk and smiled back at him before looking at a restaurant across the road. Morello's face fell. He was looking through the window of a joint that boasted herbal tea and vegan bean burgers.

"I'm messing with you," she said as she laughed at the obvious disappointment on his face. "I like my vegan bean burgers medium rare and made of prime beef." She turned and looked behind her at the glass frontage of a dark steak bar before judging a gap in the flow of people and stepping through. Morello followed her inside, his senses instantly assaulted by the heady aromas of sizzled meat and frying garlic butter.

No matter what advances they made in food, from the three expanding pills that formed their twenty-four-hour field rations to the reconstruction of organic material with 3D printers, nothing would ever quite replace the smell and taste of perfectly cooked ribeye.

"Now you're talkin'," he said to her as he stepped up beside her.

The floor manager-cum-waiter swept over to them, nodding to Brandt with familiarity, and gestured for her to walk in the direction he dictated. His lips pursed, and his eyebrows rose as he cast an appraising look up and down Morello's form. They sat in a booth, old red leather and dark wood surrounding them but probably all recently refurbished and carefully aged to look like an early twenty-first century steak joint.

All around them were sections of carefully exposed brickwork to give the building an authentic feel, alongside subtle screens built into shallow recesses that cycled old pictures of the steak house in various stages throughout its long history.

"I didn't know if we were going to see you again this time," he said to her in a warm but haughty tone. "Thought you'd shipped out again, but instead I see you've brought your own prime sirloin with you?"

Morello, despite himself, blushed. Brandt laughed and gave no answer.

"Or is he dessert, honey?" Brandt laughed again.

"He's a work colleague," she explained sternly as she smiled, closing off the conversation before it could devolve and embarrass the commander any more.

He held both hands up in surrender, then offered them both menus in small, leather-bound folders. Brandt didn't open hers.

"Sirloin, medium rare, sweet potato fries and a salad," she said.

"Usual for you," the waiter said. "And you, sweetie?"

Morello cleared his throat in as manly a fashion as he could manage to cover his awkwardness as he scanned down the menu. It was one of those restaurants that was so confident in its expertise that it offered few variations. He chose the most mouthwatering option, trying not to calculate the costs involved.

"Ribeye," he said as he snapped the old leather-bound menu shut. "Medium, and the same as my friend."

Forty-nine credits for a steak? Tonight's gonna cost me a couple hundred at least…

The waiter left with a flourish and a smirk to Brandt.

"You're a regular then?" he asked her.

"Yeah, I hit this place at least once every time I'm home. I like it here."

"You don't get back west much?"

She stopped and watched his face, waiting for him to realize his mistake. His face stayed resolutely unfazed.

"Why west?" she asked carefully. "Why not anywhere else?"

"Because you're not from here," Morello told her, "and your accent is—"

"My accent is a mixture and doesn't sound like the people in the town where I grew up. Didn't my *file* tell you that?" she accused him quietly.

"No," he admitted, "it didn't."

"So, are you going to tell me the real reason we're here?" she pressed, forcing him to look around and lean in closer to speak in a hushed tone.

"UNID," he said. It wasn't clear whether he was with the intelligence directorate or just acting on their behalf. "I just wanted to be sure you understood the reasons behind what happened today."

"I got busted down for screwing the pooch on an op. People died, it was my fault. I'm lucky not to be in jail. That's what happened."

"Not quite," Morello said. "I need your word that what I am about to tell you is treated as classified information. I'm sure I don't need to remind you that acting on this privileged intelligence would be seen as an act of treason against the territory…"

Brandt's eyes narrowed. She had seen the lawyer in him instantly as he used terminology like he would in a courtroom. The other curiosity was that breaching the confidentiality of the information he was willing to share with her would be seen as treason not to the UN, not to the combined territories, but to *the* territory. To the Americas. Her interest spiked and she nodded her assent.

"The terror attack on the government building in South Africa was a UNID cover," he said. Her mouth tightened on the string of obscenities she wanted to pour out. "It was a necessity. Not one I agree with if I'm honest, but the risk of discovery was too high otherwise."

He paused, looking into her eyes and waiting for any response. She said nothing.

"The African Territory government had stolen weapons tech," he went on, "and a lot of recent terror attacks have been traced to their government funding separatist groups in South East Asia and the former Middle East. That includes the attack on the lunar space port six years ago."

Her eyes went wider before narrowing in anger. He had her full attention.

"The intelligence package was intentionally misleading, but the expectation was that you would withdraw and kill the op. It was never intentioned that some of your team get killed in the blast."

"Sixty percent," she corrected softly. "Sixty percent of my team died in that bomb blast. And I just got hung out to dry for it... or did I?"

"Not really," he said. "The court martial was a routine matter as would always happen in those circumstances, because some of the reports couldn't be ignored. The UN needed their scapegoat, especially as we had subcontracted the real target to an external source."

"Outsourced SpecOps?" she asked with incredulity.

"Something like that," he admitted. "I don't have all the information on it, other than rumor that it was a former UNPF of ours.

He has the right enhancements to get the infiltration work done." Brandt dismissed that as an irrelevance.

"So, you plant the fake intel, send me and my team off on our wild goose chase, publicly demote and blame me when people died, but it was all really an elaborate plan to steal back weapons plans from a supposedly friendly territory who are at least partly behind the terrorist threat?"

"Hard to believe, huh?"

"No," she said. "Easy to believe, just disgusting. Appalling, actually." He leaned back, half expecting the swing of a fist that she nearly threw as she continued. "And on top of my people getting killed as collateral, you make *me* the scapegoat and end my career?"

"Not exactly," he said. "Until the media interest dies down, you are officially demoted and sent to guard the lunar penal facility." He spoke more quickly then, and half raised a hand to ward off her anger at the posting, "But *actually* you'll be there to on standby to rendezvous with people at our research facility."

"And what if I don't keep my mouth shut?" she asked, even if she knew she'd never turn whistle-blower. "What's to stop me going to the global media?"

"The scientist working in that facility is an old friend of yours," he told her, "and there's a realistic threat to his life and those of the rest of his team. We need you, Commander, to keep them safe and escort them to their goal. We don't have the time to vet and recruit another operative with your skills and motivation."

"What is their goal, exactly?" she asked.

"Mars," he said flatly. Brandt leaned back and took a breath. She knew that being angry with him was pointless; he was just a part of that big, shadowy machine that worked behind the scenes.

"Why me?" she asked him.

"Because UNID already knows you can be trusted," he told her. "Because they gave you the fast-track in the first place and you kept your mouth shut back then."

Suddenly it dawned on her. The death of Jake Santana and the terrorist he shot a dozen times at point blank range. The terrorist who had the ability to bounce bullets clean off him without armor.

"Also," he said with a slight smirk, "some UNID lieutenant commander wrote a glowing report about your courage and bravery and requested you be personally assigned to a covert mission."

The report handed to the admirals in her court martial flashed through her mind, the one she had not been permitted to see and had been wiped immediately afterwards.

"So, who is my new subbie?" she asked, wanting to know who in the secretive UNID thought they knew her so well.

"Lieutenant Commander Torres will meet you at our north-eastern field office at thirteen-hundred tomorrow."

Torres? Brandt's face registered shock at the information dump she had just downloaded. Their salads were brought over, and they separated from leaning their heads close to one another, both looking slightly embarrassed and amusing the waiter.

"Something to drink?" he asked.

"We'll take a bottle of Harlan Cabernet," she said with a wicked smile. The waiter raised his eyebrows almost to his immaculately styled hairline and spun away theatrically.

"Harlan? What's that? Red? Californian?"

"It's two hundred credits a bottle," she said deadpan. "Bill it to the UNID."

CHAPTER 11

UNID American Field Office, Worcester, Massachusetts

"Comma—" Brandt stopped herself and amended her new rank. "*Lieutenant* Commander Brandt here for Lieutenant Commander Torres," she told the desk clerk, a gray-jacketed woman who would probably have described herself as the first line of defense. She was a bitch, Brandt thought. No two ways about it.

"Have a seat," Brandt was told and treated to a smile so false that it almost seemed like a threat, as though she dared the disgraced officer to disobey her. The woman stood and walked away from the desk, revealing that the jacket matched the pants she wore.

Brandt turned and sat on one of the uncomfortable-looking padded benches in the wide, double-heighted reception area. Despite appearances, her ass sank into the cushions just the right amount and she found herself relaxing despite the hostile reception that anyone not in the UNID got.

As instructed, she had arrived wearing civilian clothing, but unlike most UNPF personnel who signed on for life, not everything about her was like a uniform. From the way she carried herself to the haircut she wore, her appearance never screamed professional soldier unless she intended it to. She had found that skill obvious when training for the CP teams. Others had walked around among civilians appearing for anyone who cared to look exactly like soldiers on a mission. Even worse, their stiffness and alertness drew attention in the worst way.

Brandt leaned back, relaxing and not looking ready to snap to attention if required. She cocked one ankle over the other knee and jigged a little, glancing around as though she had all the time in the world to take in the sights. For ten minutes she practiced the skill of social invisibility, just for the fun of developing something small and personal, until her fidgeting made her unnoticeable in the flow of people coming and going.

A harsh buzzer sounded and she glanced causally toward her left, seeing a familiar yet older face emerge from the reinforced frosted glass entrance to the heart of the building.

Tall with broad shoulders, a triangular shape to his upper body, and with an immaculately groomed short beard, was Lieutenant Commander Torres. The young boy she had known, barely hitting puberty when they'd last laid eyes on one another, had grown into a fit and confidant young man. His elevation to lieutenant commander when most men his age would still be looking at half a decade in the rank of lieutenant spoke something of his abilities, she guessed, or at least his connections.

Brandt stood, locking eyes with the young man and seeing a mischievous sparkle in them as he approached. The two shook hands when he got near enough and she smiled at up him, half a head taller than her.

"Look who grew up," she quipped with a smirk. "How you doin', Torres?"

"I'm good," he said with an air of confidence that the younger incarnation hadn't possessed.

"You've been better though, right?"

"You can say that again."

"Walk with me," he told her, striding back toward the glass door where he held the inside of his left wrist to a shining panel in the wall. Green lights blinked subtly, and the door slid open. Torres walked in and held up a hand to the two armor-suited guards who stepped forward to challenge the unauthorized person who followed him inside. The door slid shut with a hiss and a slight atmospheric pop which made her glance back behind her to see the atrium in full detail, when the view from the opposing side had been impenetrable. That was how the guards knew she hadn't scanned herself in, she realized.

"She's with me," Torres said firmly.

"Yes, sir," one of the faceless visors responded through the speakers in the faceplate.

"You'll have to sign her in."

Torres ignored the obvious instruction and swiped on the large datapad before tapping various commands into it. Brandt looked at the guards, who still maintained a careful watch on her. They wore the new type of armor that she had briefly owned; the slight variations and reduced thickness of the plates were obvious to her trained eye.

Priority in bureaucracy as ever, she thought. *Well-funded departments ahead of front-line units like always.*

"Brandt," Torres said, snapping her out of her wandering thoughts and back to the present. She looked to see him gesturing for her to step up to the datapad.

"Preset with your biometrics," he told her. "Just need to confirm."

She placed her right hand flat on the large screen and felt it glow hot for a fraction of a second. She withdrew her hand and waited as a circular loading icon flashed at her for a few heartbeats. A message came up on the screen to confirm that she was now authorized.

"Come on," Torres said, bypassing the two guards, who reverted to their watching positions. "Let's get you plugged in to the system before we start."

Brandt wasn't sure what he meant by getting plugged in, but she followed anyway.

"I see you got the new armor here," she said as they walked. They passed through high corridors with frosted glass walls on either side.

"Last year," he answered. "You never saw it before?"

"I got a suit on CP," she said before grimacing and correcting herself. "Or at least I *had* a set. I had to book it back in when I got brought home after…"

"I know. It's waiting to be shipped up to the lunar base. I meant you'd never seen it before you got it on CP." Torres told her. She smiled.

"Really?"

"God's honest," he answered with a disarming smile. "You'll have to keep it stored and wear the old rig until we ship off for Mars, though."

"Awesome. And no, never knew the upgrade was a physical one until the rigs turned up. Gotta say I was very pleasantly surprised."

She frowned, thinking about something else he had said.

"Why?"

"Why what?"

"Why do I have to keep it stored until we do the red-run?" she asked.

"You're going there as a punishment, remember? The UN is hardly going to let you keep upgraded tech beyond your posting, now, are they?"

Brandt said nothing, but glared at him until he spoke.

"Low profile," he said in a placating tone. "Old armor, bad attitude and under the radar, got it?"

"Sir, yes, sir," she muttered sarcastically under her breath.

"After you," he said, stopping at an unmarked door and gesturing for her to go in ahead of him.

Two men in lab coats looked at her expectantly, one prepping a small device and walking toward a medical bench and waiting.

"On the bed, please," he said. He looked over the machine that appeared like a massively oversized old syringe. That technology had been phased out before her time with the advances in medicine, but the design was familiar.

"I already got my tetanus booster, thanks," she said. The scientist didn't laugh, just looked at Torres.

"Left forearm," he told her. "Lay on the bed or stand if you want, but some people pass out when the chip bonds to their central nervous system."

Brandt hesitated for a moment, then pulled up her left sleeve. She kept her eyes on Torres as she felt the cold, stinging crunch of the chip being physically stabbed into her flesh. She ground her teeth together as the numbing tingle of electricity shot up the nerves of her arm. A sensation of hotness crept up her neck to tickle her brain behind her nose and a sudden lurch of unsteadiness threatened to spin the room out from under her, before she blinked it away. She regained control as the feelings faded.

The lab-coated man withdrew the wide needle and sprayed a blob of clear gel onto the bleeding wound. The gel flattened itself out and formed a hard lump over her wound. No blood seeped out and the pain of the procedure went away instantly as the anesthetic wound sealant did its job perfectly.

"Cool," she said as she flexed her fingers. "Do I get free coffee now? Twenty percent off at any Chevrolet dealership?"

"Yes, actually," Torres answered, "and Ford." Brandt looked at him quizzically.

"I'm messing with you," he said. "Although you do get free coffee. That part's real."

~

She sat at the large table in the briefing room, placing her coffee cup on the expanse of dark resin in front of her. It had all the visual properties of glass but felt warm to the touch instead of the coolness it suggested. She had opened the door herself, testing out her new UNID passport that operated on a frequency not used by anyone else. She wasn't fazed by having a biometric scanner chip implanted in her body; she already had one near her spine between her shoulder blades that had been implanted, far more painfully she recalled, when she had first joined the UNPF.

She sat opposite Torres and before either of them could get into any small talk the door buzzed softly. When it clicked open, two plain-looking men entered in forgettable suits with haircuts to match. Brandt had seen these types before, six years ago after the terrorist attack on the Moon; they were UNID agents.

"I'm Curtis," one said as he sat and indicated the slightly younger one. "This is Ward." Ward nodded at her. Both men ignored Torres, already being acquainted with him.

"I'll be brief," Curtis said. "You are tasked to take a position at your newly demoted rank at the lunar penal facility in the Shackleton crater."

"Ironic," she said softly.

"Excuse me?" Curtis asked, annoyed at her interruption. "Shackleton? Shackle-town?" She looked around the room and saw only Torres suppressing a smirk. *Tough crowd.*

"You will report to Commander Franks," Curtis said, ignoring her interruption, "and you will adopt that role until such time as any media interest in you and the incident in South Africa dies down. Something tells me it won't be long…" His eyes met Ward's and the two shared a cruel smile. "And then what?" Brandt asked.

"Then you will be quietly reassigned to a ship's guard detail and travel to our facility on Mars. You are to be contactable and on standby to relocate at all times."

"Easy as that?"

Curtis glared at her. "Let's make something abundantly clear to you, *Lieutenant* Commander. You are here only because others have vouched for you and used influence higher up the chain of command in UNID to save your ass. We were happy to throw you in jail, in the very facility you are being sent to work in. Think yourself lucky and show a little goddamned gratitude."

Brandt smiled, despite the slight shock she had received. These guys were powerless to make her life uncomfortable; Curtis had admitted as much when his temper got the better of him and he disclosed that there was a bigger fish in the pond with a personal interest in her.

"Oh, I do," she said, leaning forward to sip her coffee before carefully putting it down. "I feel blessed to have been made your scapegoat after you had almost all of my team killed to cover up some shady op you couldn't have in the official books. I am *so* grateful that you are publicly punishing me for part of your cover story. Thank you."

Torres cleared his throat and sat up, wanting to head off the conversation before people stood up and raised their voices, peacocking until there was no recourse other than violence.

"The admiral made her wishes clear, gentlemen," he reminded them. Curtis shot him a withering look and paused to gather himself before continuing.

"The operation conducted by our subcontractors was vital to global security," he went on, "and we had to get the plans back from the factions inside the UN territory government who would misuse it."

"What plans?" Brandt asked. "What's this new tech you're keeping secret?"

"It's need-to-know," Curtis said as he stood, "and you don't need to know." The line was weak, but he exercised every part of his small power over her. "You ship out tonight at twenty-three fifty."

He exited with Ward following, leaving Brandt and Torres alone in the room.

"What admiral," she asked with narrowed eyes, "would take an interest in saving my ass?"

Torres blushed slightly before answering, his eyes looking anywhere but at hers.

"Admiral Torres," he finally confessed.

CHAPTER 12

Earth's Upper Atmosphere

"Stand by for burn in three, two, one... mark."

The sound of the pilot's voice was crisp in her ear. It was distorted only by the sound of their small transport ship rumbling and roaring as it forced its way out of the invisible field of gases sealing the Earth off from the black void beyond. The helmet of her suit—her old suit and not the new tech she missed already—was clipped to her waist. She couldn't bear the stuffy interior for the few hours of flight. She glanced down at her right shoulder; the wide stripe of gold paint had been poorly scrubbed away and replaced with fresher paint bearing a triangle of three stars to denote her new rank.

She had had the same feeling at various points in her career, recalling the pride when the single vertical stripe had become two on her first promotion, then again when it had become a single star when she entered the officer training academy and onward through the ranks until the badge of commander was emblazoned on her chest and shoulder. Somehow the poor job in removing that rank symbol stung her even worse than the reality of being demoted and being sent to perform a menial task. Now she'd just have to suck it up and wait for her turn.

The sound and vibration abated as they passed through the atmosphere and out into the black calm beyond. Brandt settled back into her uncomfortable seat, looking around at the other UNPF troops assigned to relief duties on the lunar surface.

They all wore their full armor suits. As none of them came close to outranking her even with her new lower status, they shot her cautious glances until she caught them looking and forced them to look elsewhere. None of them could hold her gaze, even from behind a visor.

They knew who she was. They had all seen the news bulletins on Global Television Networks when they aired a piece outside the UN headquarters following her court martial. She knew the other troops would find their courage eventually and was glad that their faces were hidden so that she didn't have to see their looks of distaste. She settled back and waited for it. It only took less than an hour.

"You know? I had a buddy on CP…" one said to the suited seaman beside him.

"Yeah?"

"Yeah," the voice came through the suit speakers loudly, clearly for her benefit to overhear. "Got himself blown up by some useless *track* who had no business being in command of anything bigger than a canteen."

"You don't say?" his co-conspirator replied.

"Sure do. He said he never liked her and knew he'd get himself killed one day because of her."

Brandt fought to keep her face still and not respond. It didn't take long before she lost the battle with herself and turned on them.

"Your buddy have a name, Petty Officer Class One?" she asked, standing and crossing the gap to where he sat trying not to cower away from her.

"No, ma'am," he stammered.

"So, he had no name? This buddy of yours real?"

He said nothing, quailing under the anger he didn't expect to face.

"So what was his name?"

"I... I..." he stammered, unable to lie and make up anything quickly enough.

"What's *your* name?"

"Hawkins, ma'am," he said.

"And you?" she snapped, turning her head to the right to take in the co-conspirator who dared to believe that he had escaped her attention.

"Brown, ma'am."

"Hawkins and Brown," she repeated, as though she was committing their names to memory for some later revenge. "What are your orders?"

"Relief guard of six for lunar penal facility," Hawkins muttered. Brandt smiled.

"Me too, Hawkins, me too." She leaned back away from him and deflated a fraction, giving him the false sense that she was no longer out for blood. "None of the CP members who died on that op would be seen dead rubbing shoulders with you, Hawkins. You know why?"

Hawkins just shook his head weakly.

"Because we didn't suffer fools or assholes, and you're both. Shut your mouth and wait to dock; I'll deal with you when I have time."

~

Lunar Arrivals had changed a lot since she had first laid eyes on it over six years before. Back then it had been a rough shed of a place inside a tough, thickly walled double-skinned dome.

There was very little in the way of commercial comfort back then; it was rudimentary and functional to the barest of minimum standards, not like the many domestic and inter-territory arrivals ports back on Earth. The whole feel back then had been like a pioneer mining station.

That had all changed.

The Moon's population grew rapidly each week as more and more people were brought up to fill the vast, empty spaces created by the new shield areas. These shields, covering the circumference like large blisters, penetrated far below the surface and interlocked to give almost seventy percent coverage. Under these shield domes were physical ones, but not designed to maintain pressurized atmosphere. Each dome followed the same geodesic pattern and was linked to the planetary core processor facility, which maintained the gravitational units and mimicked the Earth's twenty-four-hour day. It didn't matter that the orbital patterns and size of the satellite differed enormously from their home planet, because science had found a way to trick anyone into believing that they were back there.

The domes projected the sunrise and the sunset, mimicked changing weather patterns and even produced infrared beams of light. This simulated sunlight made anyone walking below them feel right at home with the sun on their backs as they worked.

A lot of the work carried out on the Moon's surface was agricultural. The enhanced and modified dirt was used to create vast fields of crops, which fed the population fresh produce and fed the animals raised there. There were science and research laboratories, and even entire domes dedicated to vacation resorts.

The climate of these was managed and modified to recreate the beating sun and humidity of popular spots back on Earth, just as others maintained the artificially created snow and ice for those who wanted winter sports. Whole bodies of water had been created, being held by other shields designed and installed to make space for diving and sailing, and all catering to the rich and influential. Last year, they had even built a sports complex complete with a football stadium.

Brandt recalled that initially there was a thought to divide up the Moon into four sections, one for each territory, but the decision was made to unify them and to claim the Moon as joint property of everyone on Earth. In doing so, many nationalities mixed together all over the parts that had been colonized. The Moon's civilization was powered by the massive singularity engines built on Earth and transported up to provide the power equivalent to thousands of the old nuclear reactor plants.

UN personnel and civilians working for the territories all enjoyed vast discounts on the resorts as almost all of them were government owned, but the Moon had also become a dumping ground for the detritus nobody wanted on Earth. The Shackleton penal facility, the only one of its kind on the lunar surface, filled a vast crater near to the south pole and housed over a hundred thousand convicted criminals ranging from corporate fraud to triple homicide. Those one hundred thousand were segmented into ten blocks which ranged out from the central hub where the kitchens, main medical services, incoming and outgoing transports all happened. Each of those ten blocks was presided over by a commander.

Brandt paused a moment to imagine what the journey would have been like, had Torres's mother not intervened at his behest and saved her ass from a ten-year jail sentence or worse. Now she simply had to suffer the temporary indignation of her shame until such time as she could get back to work doing what she did best. She still had no idea how long that would be, but as she had to maintain her cover, Torres flew separately to the Moon with a promise to meet up with her inside of a week.

Stepping out into Lunar Arrivals along with the rest of the general population, Brandt was annoyed that there was no separate UNPF arrivals and departures port. If there was, she hadn't been sent to it. She waited in line, her massive kit bag held easily over one shoulder thanks to the powered armor she still wore, and shuffled forward until called to immigration control. The booth was staffed by a young man in the black uniform of the CTSC, the combined territories security company that had replaced much of UNPF combined territory forces roles off-world in recent years. It had always been cheaper to outsource to private companies than to waste the manpower and training hours on creating soldiers only for them to guard doors in some freezing corner of the Moon.

The exception to that rule, evidently, was the penal colony.

"ID," the bored-sounding voice rattled off at her, "and the nature of your visit to the lunar colonies."

Brandt swept her left forearm over the reader, being as subtle as she could be, just to see if it worked. The datapad in front of the man stayed silent and blank.

Worth a try, she thought.

"Brandt, Leslie. Lieutenant Commander UNPF posted to lunar penal facility." The rent-a-guard tapped at his screen, gesturing without looking for her handprint on the grubby-looking scanner on her side of the booth. She shuddered internally, dropping her bag to unclip and remove her right gauntlet. She made no show of hiding her annoyance and disdain as she pressed her palm to the glass.

"You disinfected this thing recently?" she asked as the lights roamed up and down her flat hand as it scanned her. He ignored her.

"Welcome to the lunar colonies," he said, his tone of voice utterly at odds with the gleeful words he read off the screen. "On behalf of the lunar government and the CTSC we wish you a safe and happy experience off-world. Any applications for inter-territory visas for your return to Earth are to be directed to the information desk after you pass through security. Have a nice day."

"Dude," she said, "did you just give me the vacation welcome line?"

He deigned to look up at her and tear his eyes away from his screen, red rings round his eyes, and just shrugged before calling for the next in line.

Brandt made no attempt to be quick about putting the gauntlet back on before picking up her bag, keeping the line stationary for almost twenty seconds and incurring shouts from further back that she was holding people up. She walked off, waiting in another line to pass through the security checkpoint. At least here her armor and rank made her feel less of a peasant. An older man with gray hair showing out from under his black uniform cap waved her forward to a wide gate at the side of the checkpoints.

"Lieutenant Commander," he said with a nod. He swiped the gate with an access card and stood back for it to swing open. Brandt thanked him as she walked though, noting the way he held himself and imagining him to have been a petty officer at least before he had ended up in private security.

"Know where you're going?" he asked her. She tapped at the wrist screen, hating the loss of her new suit even if it was temporary, and showed him the quarters designation she had been given.

"South train goes underground most of the way there," he told her. "Get off at Callan Station and take the old overland. It's a lot nicer that way because you get to go through the cornfields. Feels like home."

Brandt thanked him again, committing the route to memory as she walked and looked overhead at the signs for the directions the shuttle trains went away from the arrivals port in. She walked, people moving around her like water around a stone. She drew some looks, but people off-world were obviously accustomed to seeing men and women in powered armor suits roaming the surface.

She saw bars, casinos, food outlets and more than one shady entrance that she wasn't sure she wanted to know any more about. It was clean—at least it was well maintained—but she felt a little dirty, like the place was infecting her with its seedy nature. She saw the rolling sign for the south train and veered off, taking the moving staircase down a level and feeling the rush of cold from the air-conditioned tunnels below.

She walked through the turnstiles, her bag getting stuck and annoying her with the sound of a small rip as she pulled it through behind her.

She waited on the platform with the other passengers, many of them lugging heavy bags unless they had spent fifty credits on hiring the expensive repulser carts to take the weight for them.

Or powered armor, she thought. *That helps.*

She waited, glancing up occasionally to watch the time of the next train arriving ticking down to one, then peered down the tunnel expecting to hear the rush of air as the train approached. Her bearings were all off. The train approached from behind her and not the direction she expected, making her re-evaluate which way she thought she had landed when the transport ship had docked. She climbed aboard, taking up the majority of the two narrow seats with her bulky armor and the entire two seats opposite her with her bag. Even then she had to sit at an angle so that her legs weren't stuck fast against the opposite row. She had had the same problem on public transport back on Earth, even without armor on.

The journey took her almost forty-five minutes, during which time she stared blankly out of the window at nothing as the train hurtled through the unlit tunnels deep underground. She knew—most of the passengers didn't—that these trains went outside of the shielded areas. Even so far underground they were still vulnerable to the lack of atmosphere, so the leading compartment on every one of the trains was huge. It had to contain a shield array capable of shrouding the entire length of it. They were the same shield emitters that escorted the heavy troop transport ships. These shields were configured for length, however, and not to encompass an attacking unit.

Had she not been paying attention, she would have missed the part where the train reached the end of a long and gentle incline. The blackness seen through the window gave way to a dull gray of a predawn, an artificial one but one all the same. The train began to decelerate rapidly to push her back into the seat. The scrolling display running lengthways along the carriage showed the approach to Callan Station. Brandt readied herself to stand and pick up her bag.

She got off, again with the crowds steering clear of her despite the fact that she was unarmed, and walked off the platform back to the main station.

Named after one of the former presidents who had either donated money or had been a big supporter of lunar expansion, the station wasn't big by any real stretch of the imagination. It was a quarter of the size of the main arrivals train platforms. She glanced around, spotting the departures board displayed high up on one plain wall. She found the train to the lunar penal facility, and checked the departure time against the time display on her forearm screen. The screen had automatically switched to a dual display to show the time back at her Earth departure point. Seeing that she had almost half an hour to kill, she went in search of the thing she liked most.

Coffee.

A vendor tried to get her to take a pastry to go with the frothy cup of caffeine-infused sugar and succeeded with surprising ease. She sat on a low wall—the flimsy bistro chairs wouldn't support the weight of her suit—and sipped the coffee in between taking bites of the pastry. Both were good, which surprised her, and when she had finished, she found her eyes casting around at the new and unfamiliar environment.

None of this had existed when she was there last. In fact, she hadn't even gotten out of the barracks or the arrivals port as it had been back then. She knew that the last few years had seen huge developments on and under the Moon's surface. How it had managed to get dirty in that time was beyond her understanding, but she guessed that the appetites of the men sent there to work in hazardous conditions for six days a week needed to be met somehow. That meant booze, women and gambling, she guessed, as even there so far away from the arrivals port there were at least three massage joints she could see from where she sat.

Neon seemed to have made a comeback there, and she was reminded of an attempt to recreate Times Square, albeit badly. Everywhere she looked there was a concentration of people and commerce. Her train arrival time neared, and she stood. An automated cleaning bot watched as she dropped the wrapper and paper cup into a nearby bin. The thing seemed to regard her for a brief moment, before bobbing its articulated arm as if to nod to her thanks for not dropping it on the deck.

"You're welcome," she told it, earning a confused look from a woman sitting nearby. The stranger quickly looked away when she realized she was staring at a soldier wearing armor and talking to herself.

The guard at arrivals had been right. The train ride over the surface was much nicer than being underground all the way there. Brandt stared out of the window and watched the artificial sun rising over the fields. It did remind her of home, even though she knew it was all an illusion. It reminded her of leaving in the night and taking a train from the west coast to travel down to the Carolinas to start her basic training and waking up to see field after field of crops passing by outside her window.

The short journey gave her a sense of peace, so when she arrived at the end of the line at the penal facility she was serene and ready to face the next round of shit she had to deal with.

Striding in to the complex she walked up to the main reception desk and asked for directions to the accommodation block, passing two very guilty and awkward-looking troops in their armor.

"Hawkins. Brown," she said in mild greeting, ignoring their salutes as she walked straight past them wearing a smile.

CHAPTER 13

Shackleton Penal Facility, Lunar Surface

"The thing you need to understand, Brandt," the fleshy and instantly unlikeable face of Commander Franks said, "is that the men here won't respect you. You have to earn that first." Brandt said nothing, just sat semi-rigid in the uncomfortable chair facing the fat man's desk for her welcome speech. "You see, they all heard what happened back on Earth, and quite frankly, they don't like it. They don't want their officers to have a track record of getting the boys and girls killed, now, do they?"

"No, sir, I don't imagine that they do."

He stopped and glared at her, annoyed that she'd interrupted to answer his rhetoric.

Perhaps, he thought, *that's why she screwed up; no understanding of the nuances of command.* He went on, recovering his thoughts.

"The boys like to know that their officers are smarter than they are, that they're a cut above, if you like... that way, they trust us when we make them work hard or our orders put them in harm's way."

Brandt thought nothing of the sort. She trusted that her officers had always trained, studied and thought harder than she had, on top of being in possession of more and better intelligence and information than she had.

Rank, and power for that matter, all came down to information, in her opinion.

She said nothing, annoying Franks again that she failed to recognize when she should and shouldn't agree with him.

"I'll start you off light," he told her, "and put you in charge of a small unit with a dedicated team. Don't want you getting your panties in a twist on one of the big cellblocks, now, do we?"

The look she fixed him with failed to penetrate the armor of his arrogant misogyny.

"Report there directly and I'll ask young Mister Dawes to show you the ropes. Should only take but a minute, honey."

"No, sir," she said, interrupting him as politely as possible.

His face changed, and he dropped whatever manners he was feigning. "No? Now, allow me to lay some goddamned protocol on you, Brandt," Franks said as he leaned forward with his elbows on the desk. His look had gone from arrogant to overtly hostile. "*I* am a commander. *You* are a lieutenant commander and since my ass is being saddled with your sorry ass, *I* tell *you* what to do, and *you* say 'yes, sir.' That understood?"

"Yes, sir," Brandt replied seriously. "However, if the commander would like to double check regulations for non-wartime deployment of UN troops to domestic and off-world taskings, then the commander would know that I am overdue a statutory rest period of between eight and eleven hours depending on the distance between my posting and my barracks. As I have been on duty since my arrival at the departure terminal on Earth, and given the time in transit between Earth and this location, and taking into consideration the time difference between the two locations, I have been on duty in excess of twelve hours now. Sir."

Franks leaned back, his fleshy, pale face registering shock and anger at her words.

"So, you like quoting procedure, huh?" he growled at her. "Then learn this: the commander of a penal colony can invoke wartime protocols on any such members of the UNPF under his command at any time, given the justification of extenuating circumstances. We are short-staffed in that particular cellblock, so I am ordering you to attend your detail immediately to assist with those extenuating circumstances. That is all."

"In writing, please, sir."

"What?"

"I am eager to obey the commander's orders to invoke the extenuating circumstances clause. However, I need them in writing." She stood ready to leave just as soon as he sent her orders. "Should only take but a minute, sir," she added, barely able to stop herself from calling the fat man 'honey.'

"Fine," Franks said, tapping at his datapad with pudgy fingers as he looked down his nose, and focused. A few seconds later her comm screen, removed from the mount on her armor, beeped softly. She tapped at it and smiled.

"Thank you, sir."

She walked out, happy with the orders, which instructed her to be on-station at oh-six-hundred the following morning.

~

Ensign Dawes was one of those people who seemed to be perpetually smiling. Even working in a dark dungeon on the Moon he was upbeat, and that attitude was infectious. Brandt found herself smiling before they had even finished their introductions.

"You want coffee, ma'am? I can get you coffee."

"Is it any good?" she asked him. He grimaced.

"Not really," he admitted, "but I'm sad to say you get used to it."

Brandt sipped her coffee, realizing that Dawes was right because it really was bad.

"Tell me what we have here," she said, looking up at the display wall ready for the low down.

"Sub-unit of forty prisoners," Dawes said. "These are the... *unique* people that the commander doesn't want in the general population."

Brandt stood, picking up a datapad and dancing her fingertips across the screen.

"Rapist, murderer, rapist... kidnapping, murderer *and* a rapist, importation of narcotics, arsonist... these are some lovely young men and women you have here, Ensign."

"I know, right?" he beamed. "I'm amazed we don't have more parties."

"Who is *this* little beauty?" she asked, double-tapping the screen to display the prisoner record on the wall. Dawes looked up at it and smiled, as though he knew the punchline before the joke had been told. He reeled off the information having only seen the face on screen.

"Mary Collins," he said, switching into a good impression of a graceful southern belle. "Sweetest lil ol' lady you'll ever meet."

Brandt laughed.

"So why is sweet ol' Ms. Collins here?" she asked in an attempt at the same voice and pleasantly surprising herself.

"Initially she was sentenced to fifteen months for possession of narcotics and an unlicensed firearm," he said. "Turns out that when she hit gen-pop she had a few connections and started to run the show. Almost five hundred people on her dorm wing and they all answered to her.

"They moved her, obviously, and she just did the same thing on the next wing. And the next, and the next, and so on and so forth until they didn't know where to put her." He sighed, looking at the sweet face of her mugshot as though he lamented the loss of the woman she could have been.

"This crazy old buzzard has killed at least twelve other prisoners in here that we can prove. We couldn't prove another five but that hardly matters. She was sentenced to death, and she's got eight months left of her statutory twelve-month appeal time. She'll lose that appeal, so the woman literally has nothing to lose. Do *not* be fooled, Lieutenant Commander," he said as seriously as his twenty years of existence allowed him to be. "She will gut you like a fish, you so much as take your eye off her following anything she perceives to be a slight."

"Duly noted," Brandt said with a raised eyebrow. "Now tell me about the symbols beside each case. What do they mean?"

Dawes stood and pointed to each one he could reach.

"Full armor unlock, that's self-explanatory, daily clean, weekly clean, medication—the number beside it is how many times a day— and this one means exercise privileges."

"What's their exercise?"

"Ten minutes in the bowl," he said, tapping the screen to bring up the CCTV image of the circular outside area with walls that curved convexly.

"Okay," she said. "So what's our day-to-day?"

"Shift change at oh-seven-hundred and nineteen-hundred. Two days, two nights, two off. You have me and a team of twenty with two petty officers on top of that. That's what we're supposed to have, anyway, but some days it's half. We're pretty short staffed here, I mean we've never even had an LT on this rotation, so I've pretty much been doing that job, and the last lieutenant commander didn't exactly fit in…"

"Meaning?"

"Meaning that they couldn't quite adapt to life here. I really shouldn't say any more, ma'am."

Brandt narrowed her eyes at the boy but decided that could wait until he knew her better.

"So tell me, if you've been doing the LT's job then what does the ensign do?"

"Make coffee and look decorative, I guess?" he said with a wry smile.

~

Despite how simple Dawes tried to make it sound, the management of the segregation unit was a constant task. Over the next twelve days Brandt found herself having to pick up messes from the team working before hers, or else trying to get the unit into order before handing it over to the next. It was out of a sense of pride, despite how other teams functioned. She spent her days off responding to all the comms traffic she never got around to on her twelve-hour shifts and though she supposedly was a unit manager, she spent almost half of her time in armor walking the landings and responding to queries from the prisoners or dealing with their constant antics.

By the time she and her team had handed over and briefed the following team, who had the annoying habit of turning up a minute before their allotted time, she was getting less than six hours sleep each night. Her fitness, having been honed to a fine edge, suffered as a result.

Luckily for her, she had much farther to fall from the top until she wouldn't be fit enough to do her job, but others were beginning to look unwell as a result of working there.

The prisoners, almost all of them, took every opportunity to cause trouble for their jailers. Of the ten or so prisoners eligible for external exercise, every day at least two would try to land a cheap shot on either a guard or another prisoner. Anything in their path was fair game to be kicked or launched in some fashion. They wanted nothing more than to cause a nuisance. Those prisoners would then be taken down and returned to their cells where they would lose exercise privileges for another forty-eight hours. They knew the system better than the guards. They lived there; the ones who opened the doors just worked there for a year and a half at a time.

Every day was the same repetitive, monotonous vomit of violence and threats. Every day it was the same tricks from different cells. The cup full of piss thrown as soon as the door opened. The handful of their own shit smeared across a visor as they ran around laughing until brought to the ground and handcuffed. The dozens of cameras installed on the unit recorded every interaction. Any indication, any hint of excessive force used by the soldiers working as jailers, and the prisoners' automatic and uninfringeable right to contact counsel saw them under constant legal investigation for wrongdoing.

The cards were stacked so far against them that there was no way to take back and maintain control without an army.

After their third shift rotation, when Brandt woke up just as exhausted as when she'd gone to sleep, she penned the first of many emails she would write to the commander.

Her report was brief, but it cited half a dozen reasons why the unit and her team in particular was understaffed and over-worked.

Franks's response was to tell her to make do with what they had. That any failure by a member of her team was a personal failure on her part as she was responsible for them and their overall performance. She noted the report and its response, flagging them for the attention of Torres just in case he wasn't aware that the lunar penal facility was an incendiary device waiting for a spark.

She worked that first dayshift back, dealing with the same incidents they had every time. Brandt felt surprisingly accepted as she walked out of the office, late after the handover briefing, to see her entire team waiting for her so that she didn't have to wait for another transport. As a group, they went through armor decontamination to clear the shit and piss from their plates. As they stepped onto the shuttle platform to take them back to the hub and ultimately out of the jail, Brandt turned to her team. All she could see was the exhaustion on their faces after two days and two nights of hell.

"Next time," she said, "we try something new."

They murmured their agreement as enthusiastically as eighteen exhausted men and women could before they lapsed into silence to await their arrival at the central hub.

"What's the new thing?" the message on her left forearm screen read after the dull beep had got her attention. She glanced at Dawes, who pretended not to be aware that they were communicating. She tapped her answer and hit send.

"Not sure, but I'll find something."

CHAPTER 14

Earth to Lunar Surface Approach

"Coming up on the Moon in a little over one hour," the pilot said over the ship-wide net.

"Understood," Specter said. The comm channel activated inside his scarred head was audible only to him; it connected directly to the fine workings of his left inner ear. The sound was undetectable to anyone else, but it was crystal clear to him. He turned and paced down the interior of the Hyper transport ship, a stark contrast to the one in which Brandt had travelled some weeks before. His booted feet stepped silently on fitted carpet and not alloy plate. The chair he sat in was plush and comfortable, even before it reclined at the touch of a button to become a flat bed.

He didn't need to sleep, not at that moment and not much at all. He didn't even need to sit down but he knew that other people who still occupied their organic bodies felt more at ease when he mimicked the physical pressures of being entirely human.

"Can I ask you a question?" his co-passenger enquired politely.

He smiled at the young man. "I can't promise you'll like the answer."

"Cool," Lieutenant Commander Torres said. "Do you remember me?"

Specter looked at him, an unnatural dull neon green glow emanating from his eyes.

"Yes. You were the wheel for our squad when what happened to me... happened."

"That's right, Torres."

"Torres," Specter said, his eyes losing focus momentarily as he recalled the memorized information from deep inside his brain. "Kyle, your birthday is July nineteenth. Son of Admiral Maria Torres, currently in command of southwest America training operations. Only child. Attended OTA after completing mandatory education and signed for an extension of duty after the terror attacks on the lunar base where I... where Seaman Santana was injured. Applied for and selected by the CP directorate as lieutenant before your official service records were sealed for four years. Next record is in relation to an administrative attachment to the UNID in north America at your current rank."

"So, you *know* me then?"

"I am aware of who you are, and I am aware that you and I technically served together at the time that my body was badly injured. I do not have recollections of that event. The information I have on you is almost entirely taken from your UNPF service file."

Torres pulled a face of mild shock and leaned back, assessing the black-clad super soldier he had been loaned by their private partners.

Specter watched him right back, and stuck to the easy route of acting as robotic all the way through as his limbs and his eyes were. He represented the physical embodiment of everything the advanced biomechanical cybernetic field of science could produce, but above and beyond that he just wore it well.

For people to see him as Jake Santana now was for them to see a flawed soldier: a broken man brought back from the brink of death and repaired, never to be whole again. The very fact that he had died to become Specter, on more than one occasion as they fought to save him, made it logical to him that he should leave that old life behind and let everyone who cared about him mourn the loss.

Years of therapy had solidified that in his mind, covering over the emotional responses to stimuli, and the brain surgery to subdue and suppress the sensory parts of his mind that reacted to trauma did the rest.

He still knew who he was, deep down, or at least who had been, but it was easier for him to be the reincarnation that came without the pain and fear.

"Tell me about the mission in Cape Town," Torres said. Specter smiled, knowing that Torres had been cleared to know the information but was likely testing him.

"The request originally came from your offices, I believe," Specter said, "and the mission parameters were met satisfactorily."

"I know that part," Torres said. "How did the infiltration and extraction go?"

"The cover of an emergency responder uniform worked perfectly. Nobody questions a uniform in a crisis. The vault was precisely where it was supposed to be, as were the plans for the Fold Drive."

At the mention of the last two words Torres stiffened, as though the mere mention of the technology outside of a sealed environment was a concern. They couldn't get much more of a sterile environment than they had, being alone in the compartment aboard a private transport in the vacuum of space. The conversation lulled, as each went into his own thoughts and considered the other man's.

The hour passed in sporadic conversation, with none of the juicy subjects being discussed, before Torres sat with his head back and his eyes closed.

Specter knew he wasn't sleeping; he could see his chest rising and falling at a rate that indicated the man was still conscious, but he didn't press conversation on him. He had recognized the young man instantly from his memory of the boy he had known. This boy had seen him blown apart and killed, or at least mostly killed, before Hyper put him back together again. The young wheel had grown tall and strong, much as he himself had changed massively over the last almost seven years since they had been fighting side by side on the Moon.

Specter had evolved. Had become weaponized. He had been broken down and re-imagined in a way that nobody could fully understand, and he wanted to use the abilities they had given him.

The channel came to life inside his ear once more as the pilot gave the standard approach calls. Their transport didn't wait in a holding position but instead flew to the southern region of the gray orb to slow and descend vertically toward a shielded arrival port. This one wasn't open to the general public. It wasn't marked on any map, nor even was it used by the CTSC or the UNPF. The size of the hangar was massive in comparison to the transport ship that arrived there, and with no visible bay doors it looked just like a hole in the ground.

"Modulating shield frequency, standby…" came the pilot's voice in his head. "Shield frequency matched—comin' in."

Lights blinked inside the bay, illuminating the landing spot detailed for them. The sleek transport glowed slightly as it passed through the invisible shield barrier. Next, the sound of the landing skids settling onto the surface clanged through the fuselage. All the while their progress was tracked by six quad-barreled miniguns, which automatically followed the transport's every movement as it came in to land.

The whine of the singularity engine winding down left a slight ring in their ears before the door popped and opened with a mechanical grind. The steps extended from the door as it folded down vertically, and the sound of the main cargo ramp at the rear descending echoed back to Torres as he stepped out.

A familiar face met him with a grin.

"Wheel! They let you out to play?" Torres smiled, ignoring the goading, and shook the man's hand.

"*Doctor* Paterson," he said.

"*Lieutenant Commander*, Torres," Paterson said back in an equable tone. "How you been, Kyle?"

"You know," Torres answered as they walked toward the hangar exit. "Gettin' by. Still fighting the good fight."

"Yeah," Paterson laughed. "Sure."

"How is the project coming along?"

"We've had a few… *setbacks*," Paterson answered. "What kind of setbacks?"

"The kind where I'm reluctant to agree to human trials. The kind where the mouse we sent through got turned inside out and we're still cleaning up the mess kind of problems."

Paterson walked in silence, leaving his words to sink in. When he had returned to Earth years ago he had expected his reward for saying nothing to be a discharge and a scholarship, instead he found himself sponsored by the UN and a private contractor who had need of a physicist they knew they could trust. Paterson was still a soldier first, but a trusted scientist second.

His work on the research teams alongside the Hyper scientists had been invaluable to the UNID; so much so that their breakthroughs had to be moved off world to keep them away from the prying eyes of other territories who weren't entirely to be trusted.

"How close are we?" Torres enquired almost betraying his nerves.

"To a ship trial? Close. The matter transporters are functional, apart from the organic matter issue, that is." Paterson paused, seeing the oddly fluid movement of an athletically slim man approaching from behind Torres.

"Well paint me pink and call me Susan," he said quietly as his mouth hung open. "He looks just like…"

"Specter, meet Doctor Paterson. He specializes in the jump technology we discussed."

Paterson shook Specter's hand, marveling at the sheer power and strangely inhuman feel to it.

"Doctor," Specter said to the dumbstruck man, "you probably remember me from who I was before. It's to be expected, so please don't be alarmed. Part of me is Jake Santana, but I have undergone significant changes so that only some of his memories remain."

"You… *Jake?*"

"As I said, Doctor, only a part of Jake remains." He hesitated, looking at Torres. "Are you happy for me to brief the doctor?"

"Bring him up to speed, by all means."

"Doctor Paterson, you have to understand that as you were studying after leaving this place years ago, I was rebuilt biomechanically. Parts of my brain are synthetic. I have some memories belonging to Jake, but I had to learn how to walk and communicate again as though I was a young child."

Paterson just gawped at him.

"But… so you're *not* Jake?"

"I'm sorry, Jamie," Specter said. "Not in the way that you knew him."

~

The small team that came with Specter took their equipment to the lab and quarters set aside for them. Everywhere he went, a team of technicians had to be close by to monitor and maintain him, making him effectively the most expensive human-operated machinery in the galaxy.

Torres nodded to a detail of five CP personnel, the large man who was their leader nodding back, and left them to their assigned task.

He dumped his operational gear in the room assigned to him, including his personal weapon loadout and two sets of armor—one his own and the other Brandt's—and took a smaller bag to the train terminal. UNID types were never questioned about where they were going and what they were doing. Torres was no exception.

Dressed in civilian clothing but carrying one of the new Hyper 6mm tactical pistols with the singularity energy cell in a holster tucked behind his back, he took the train toward the main hub on the southern hemisphere. Torres walked out of the train station with the other passengers to join the flow of people and checked into a cheap hotel above one of three casinos on the promenade.

These kinds of run-down, watch-your-back sort of areas were everywhere on the lunar surface, and all manner of people came and went between them.

"How many nights?" the bored desk clerk asked as Torres walked in.

"Give me two for starters," Torres said. His words and demeanor were no longer that of a soldier but of someone a little darker, maybe even more dangerous.

"Eighty credit deposit," she said in her nasal voice, "and forty-three a night."

Torres knew when he was being hustled, but he played along just enough so that their interaction was normal, and he didn't make himself too memorable. For him to walk in and just pay the asking price would mark him as a man with money to burn. He couldn't attract attention.

"Fifty," he countered as he drew actual cash from his pocket, "and thirty-five a night, with ten to you if we skip the registration forms."

She regarded him, more bored than intrigued.

"Make it a twenty, and okay."

He counted out the money, dropping it on the desk before deliberately siding one of the notes toward her. She ignored him, snatching up the cash and stuffing it inside her bra before sliding him a keycard and counting out the rest.

"Room eight, second floor, *Mister Smith*," she said sarcastically.

Torres took the stairs up to the landing above, glad that he had chosen this place. All reputable hotels asked their guests to register a biometric scan to be coded to their room's security. No such gadgetry with this place—just a plain, old-fashioned keycard, which he waved over the reader of room eight.

The door clicked open and he paused, looking around to be sure that nobody watched him. He tried again, shutting the door and swiping his left forearm over the reader to be rewarded with the same result. He smiled, happy that the trojan software installed with lock manufacturers was proving to be a good investment. He entered the room, glancing around at the sterile décor. A room this sparse would be quick and easy to clean. Another way for the hotel to stay cheap. The bed was hard, which wasn't a bad thing in his opinion, and at least the covers *looked* clean.

He dropped his bag on the bed and pulled out his datapad to tap on the screen and access the communications network. He used his own account to access the shift rotations and personnel lists at the penal facility, then opened another program to send a message. He didn't encrypt it. There was no point; the facility he was sending it to had more holes than a golf complex. Instead, he kept the message content safe.

"On lunar surface," it said, "meet me at Finnegan's, south promenade nearest your location, at twenty-one-hundred tonight. Your round."

CHAPTER 15

Lunar South Promenade Twelve

"Finnegan's, Finnegan's…" Brandt said to herself absent-mindedly as she walked along the promenade. She saw rough men loitering against walls and women dressed in neon lingerie outside some bars and massage parlors to entice the people inside. Most of the underworld activity here stemmed from the flow of UNPF credits, she knew, as this was the closest place to where hundreds of them lived and worked in poor conditions. It was only natural that they would need to let off a little steam once a week.

Brandt wore boots and tight jeans, with a dark tan jacket over a thin sweater against the chillier temperature. She made no attempt to look like she was just there to browse. It was obvious that she was new to the place, given how she stared too long at just about everything. She wasn't there covertly anyway; she was simply meeting a friend for a drink.

"You lookin' for somewhere, honey?" a gruff voice asked from beside her. She turned to see a very stocky man, borderline overweight but heavily muscled underneath, with his wide, bare arms sticking out from the rolled-up sleeves of a shirt. His face bore a handful of small scars, no doubt mementos of numerous bar fights, but his eyes were clear blue and shone with intelligence.

"Finnegan's," she said, looking him in the eye without faltering.

"Up there a ways," he told her. "Look for the green neon. But wouldn't you want to go somewhere a little better? Nice lady like you?" She pursed her lips, not taking the bait.

"I'm sure I'll survive," she assured him.

"Because it's full of people drinkin' and gamblin'," he said with mock surprise, "and that's what you'd call a sin."

"I'll bear that in mind," she laughed. "Thanks."

She found Finnegan's easily after another hundred paces, under a bright green neon sign bearing the name. The brightness on the outside didn't follow to the inside when she ducked through the door into dark wood and low lighting. The ceiling was artificially low, probably to recreate the quaint Irish pub it was based on. She didn't stop to look around for Torres. Instead, she walked up to the bar and grabbed herself a stool at the farthest end. Her training had kicked in long before she walked inside, and she sat waiting to catch eyes with the barman. In the interval, she kept the restrooms visible to her right and the exit visible ahead. The barman wasn't busy, but he kept her waiting a moment longer than she liked.

"Hey, buddy," she said in a tone of voice that implied she wasn't the kind of woman to be left waiting.

"What can I get for you, m'dear?" he asked her with a smile as false as a tin medal, in an Emerald Isle accent that was equally as believable.

"Beer and a bourbon," she said, ignoring the look he gave her for not requesting Guinness or an Irish whisky.

He knocked the cap off a brown bottle and slapped a wide glass down on a napkin next to it, pouring a generous splash into it before restoring the bottle to a high shelf.

The bartender walked back up the bar without another word to Brandt. She rested her elbow on the bar and held the neck of the bottle, swirling the liquid inside and feeling the drops of condensation running between her fingertips. The slight scrape of a chair being pushed back zeroed her attention to the right side of the bar, but she didn't follow it with a look. Instead she lifted herself up to pour the beer into her mouth and turned to catch the angle in the mirror behind the bar. Slightly distorted and obscured by bottles, she saw the tall frame of Torres walked toward the bar.

Brandt watched as he waited for the barman, who probably called himself Seamus or Patrick, to notice him. She took another pull of her beer and kicked back the bourbon before making a small sound of satisfaction and putting the glass back down with a knock on the wooden bar.

"What'll it be, friend?" Seamus asked Torres.

"I'll take a Guinness," he said, a slight slur in his words as he leaned heavily against the bar. "And another drink for the lady," he finished, leaning back to regard her and grin.

His Guinness was poured, the creamy-white foam swirling until it turned black from the bottom of the glass upward. Brandt had another beer and another splash of bourbon tipped into her glass, which she raised to him in thanks. Taking that as the sign of encouragement, he slid himself along the bar. He seemed to have already consumed a few of the alcoholic protein shakes he was drinking by the pint, and climbed up on another stool beside her.

"Hi," he said.

"Hi. You been here long?"

"A while," Torres said with a childish grin.

"I take it you aren't working then?"

"Oh, I am…" he said, pausing to gulp his drink and turning back to her with a cream-colored froth moustache. He screwed up his features in disgust at the drink and set it down before declaring loudly, "This is swill. I wouldn't give this to a dog to drink."

Silence fell over the dozen muted conversations going on in the bar.

"Keep your voice down," Brandt hissed, misunderstanding his level of drunkenness.

"That'll be your last then, friend," the barman said in hostile tone. "You can be on your way now."

"I mean, how is it so hard to make it taste like it does in Ireland?" Torres said more loudly, ignoring both warnings that he had just received. "This is *shit*."

The barman looked over Torres's shoulder and two men stood to approach. Both were tall, but one was huge, easily as big as the man Brandt had spoken with outside. Torres stood, unsteady on his feet but his left hand fluttered behind his back and came out holding a pistol to her that nobody else could see. She hesitated for a split-second before she took it and slipped it inside her jacket.

"And who the hell are you two?" he said as he staggered backward and righted himself.

"Oh, er, well I'm Martin," the smaller one said politely and sarcastically in a Boston accent, "and this here is my brother, Tommy. Say hi, Tommy."

Tommy smiled at Torres and slapped him hard across the face, taking his knees out from under him and making him fall against the bar. Brandt went to move but he held a hand out, invisible to anyone but her. She waited.

"Wait, hold up," Torres said as he stood again wearing a grin like he was the guy's number one fan. "Tommy Fallon? *The* Tommy Fallon?"

The two men stopped and looked at each other in confusion. That moment of hesitation was all it took.

Torres kicked out, stamping a boot straight into Tommy's groin and following it up with a savage swing of his cupped hand to clap the big man's left ear. Tommy went down, hitting the deck just as his brother managed to react. His hand disappeared inside his jacket but never got a chance to come back out—Torres clamped his elbow tight to the man's body and grabbed the back of his head to slam it down onto the bar. The crunch of bone echoed under the low ceiling. As the barman came up from a crouch to level a gun at Torres, Brandt appeared holding the gun he had slipped her.

She didn't recognize the type of weapon, but that hardly mattered. It had only a few working parts and one of those had her right index finger curled lightly around it.

"Put it down," she snapped. "Put it down *now*."

The barman slowly took his hand away from the weapon and held it out to his side. Torres took the gun, a pump-action shotgun that wouldn't have just killed him. It would have dismembered him. He spoke in a voice that wasn't nearly as drunk as he had been making out.

"Kappa One, move in."

The light coming from the door was blocked out as four men moved in, weapons in their hands. The big guy Brandt had spoken to outside walked straight up to Torres.

"Couldn't wait for us?"

"Spur of the moment thing," Torres replied. "Bag and tag these assholes for me."

"You got it."

"And don't forget Seamus here, too," Brandt said after lowering the pistol from where she pointed it at the barman's head.

"My name's Graham," he said, dropping the feigned accent as quickly as he had dropped the shotgun.

"Graham as well then," she said.

The CP team moved in, led by the big man she had seen further down the promenade. They scooped up the suspects and their collaborator before checking the IDs of everyone else in the bar. None of their biometric scans flagged, so the team left with just three prisoners.

Brandt turned to Torres.

"Worst date ever," she complained. "Couldn't have done that *before* I arrived?"

"Check your watch," he told her, sipping his Guinness again.

She did. It showed twenty-fifty-nine.

"You're early."

"So, you really aren't here to rescue me from jail?" she asked him over a drink.

They had moved to the farthest end of the promenade away from Finnegan's. Torres had assured her that the threat was minimal, but that they had a lead on a pair of guys wanted for questioning and he decided to tag the mission on to him getting to the Moon anyway. It all added to his cover.

"Sadly not, no parole for you just yet. You met Franks?"

Brandt's sneer told him that she had, which made him laugh.

"You know, it was my mother who posted him there four years ago."

"Four years? And he hasn't been rotated back yet?"

"No, and he won't be. She gave him the option to resign his commission or she'd personally post him. He stuck to his guns and so did she." Torres shrugged as though the stubbornness of old men was no concern of his.

"Well, he's an ass," Brandt said, "but he doesn't cause me any real problems."

"What is troubling you then?"

She sighed and ran her finger up and down the side of her beer bottle wiping marks through the condensation. "The unit I'm on," she complained. "It's grossly understaffed and the rules all bend in favor of the prisoners. They do what they want and unless one of them actually kills one of us, nothing happens. Every day we have to fight, but with both hands tied behind our backs. We wear armor, so we don't get hurt but we aren't allowed to use force back until it's already kicked off. I'm telling you, it's a matter of time before someone goes down and stays down."

Torres regarded her with something nearing amusement. "What?"

"You, caring about the cover job," he said.

"I do. There are good people there and they don't deserve the crap they have to put up with," she explained, picking at the label on her bottle.

"So what are you going to do about it? Or are you asking me to do something about it?"

"Could you pull some strings and have an extra few relief units sent up? Allow for some time off or overstaff some of the wings to clear out the bad?" she asked him hopefully.

"No," he said. "*I'm* not the admiral in my family, remember? And besides, even she couldn't because it's out of her jurisdiction by, what? Fifty million clicks?"

"Fifty-four point six," she corrected him pointlessly, "and I know. So, who is the one calling the shots?"

Torres took a long pull on his beer. Having spent less time Brandt had in service, it wasn't as though he had a wealth of experience to fall back on. What he did have were connections. He had spent most of his career either in special operations or attached to the secretive Intelligence Directorate. On top of that, he had the added bonus of having been present at more than a few working dinners where his mom, the admiral, talked shop.

"It's not like it is on Earth," he explained. "Up here it's corporate. It's business. It's entire territories investing wealth into a new frontier like some multi-billion credit land-grab from the ancient west. Up here the territories are subcontracting to the lowest bidder, just to maximize profits from the newest thing: undeveloped land." He paused to drink, getting straight back into the flow.

"I mean, come on, only a few hundred years ago we were killing each other over the last few puddles of dead dinosaur juice. Countries were literally invading their neighbors with little or no justification just to drill for the old black gold. Fast forward, and where are we? On the Moon, which is colonized, and soon we'll be heading to Mars behind the ones already there, which will probably only be thirty years behind the lunar colony in development. Our rate of expansion is unprecedented, and who knows where we'll be soon? Further than Mars, I can promise you that."

"You can?" Brandt asked him, amused by the long geo-political and socio-economic speech that came from his mouth. All she could see when his face grew earnest was the young boy she had known him as before his SpecOps chrysalis transformation.

He looked over each shoulder casually and leaned in closer to her.

"Proxima Centauri," he whispered cryptically.

"Proxima Centauri as in another solar system, Proxima Centauri?" she asked.

He shushed her.

"How?" she hissed more quietly.

"Can't tell you here," he said, "but it's not a combined territories project. It's *us*, the American UN, our UNID and private partners."

"Why?" she asked intensely. "Why risk the conflict and not share… whatever it is that means we can reach further than our own system. The scope for this is… is… *astronomical!* Literally!"

"I know," he said, hushing her with his flat palms to try and suppress the excitement. "That's why it's so far under wraps that nobody can get wind of what we're doing."

"Which is what?"

Torres pursed his lips, regretting having said too much already.

"I'm still waiting for clearance to bring you in to the last part," he told her, "but I promise that when I can, you'll be out of that jail and on the team."

"What's the holdup?"

"I haven't quite convinced our partners to sign off on it yet. Some of them have… *concerns* that you might not let what happened back on Earth slide."

Brandt's lips tightened as her eyes narrowed, letting him know exactly what she thought of that opinion.

"I get it," he told her. "Just hold fire for a little while longer, okay? And if I might, I think you need to look at the problems there from a different standpoint. Like a *legal* one?"

"Fine," she said. "I'll wait, but you tell me something else…"

He raised his eyebrows, waiting for the question. "What really happened on that operation?"

CHAPTER 16

Lunar Penal Facility

"Morning," Brandt said as Dawes called her team to attention for their morning briefing. It was their first day back after two days of rest. She hadn't rested much, given the incredible information that was burning a hole in her head. Low murmurs of greeting answered her, the air in the room becoming as depressed as the people it held. Three more of her staff were in the infirmary after their days off, and each day the UNPF troops assigned to the prison facility dropped like flies.

"Today is going to be different," she said confidently, getting their attention. "The staffing contingencies here constitute a state of emergency, legally speaking. I've checked this, and commanders are already invoking emergency procedures to ensure a change in regime and additional funding for more staff."

~

She had, in a way. She had ensured that the right information found its way to Franks's desk with instructions so simple to follow that they might as well have been written in crayon. Her late-night call to Morello had been the final piece in the puzzle. She had to admit that she'd felt a little reckless after a few drinks and had decided to wake him up to call on his legal expertise.

Using the UNID communications network which she wasn't strictly supposed to, she was able to have a real-time conversation despite the distance involved. She didn't ask how and she knew they wouldn't tell her.

Morello had been confused, discombobulated to say the least, but eventually he had relented and applied his legal mind to the problem.

"Hold on," he told her, rubbing his face as she felt a pang of guilt at his red-ringed eyes.

It was three in the morning for him, but after he had carried the datapad to the kitchen in his New York apartment and pressed the right buttons to give him coffee, he was awake. He told her he would be getting up in three hours anyway, so it was fine. She knew it wasn't and promised to make it up to him. She had laid out the problem for him and set the task, seeing him flex his neck from side to side and go to work searching for legal precedent. They chatted a little as he worked but his attention was on the task.

"Okay," he said eventually. "You got access to personnel records? Can you see current figures for injured or sick through duty?"

"Yeah..." she said as she minimized the window displaying his face and tapped at the screen. "No. I'm locked out of the current data. I can only see the completed months and only for my block. It's asking for an override authorization. Dammit."

"They fitted your UNID chip yet?" he asked her conspiratorially.

"Yeah, but I tried it at immigration and nothing happened."

"That's because it won't work on immigration. Activate biometric authority to override and try it."

She did, and her eyes went wide as her authorization was accepted. It didn't display her name and rank like her handprint did, only gave a UNID authorization code and the data appeared as available to view.

"Well, I'll be goddamned…" she muttered to herself, making Morello smile. "Got it… *whoa*—the entire facility has a thirty-six percent inefficiency rate through illness."

"There's your smoking gun," Morello said as he typed furiously. "Anything that causes a fall-off rate in excess of twenty-five percent is classed as a hazardous environment and allows a state of emergency or war to be declared. If your commander sends… *this*," he hit the screen his end and a new message icon flashed up on Brandt's screen in the top corner, "…to his superiors, then they will have kittens. He needs to copy the report to the adjutant's office, that way his command can't ignore it."

"I owe you."

"Damn right you do," he said. "You know how hard my ass got chewed for that dinner check?"

"You're a big boy, you can handle it. And anyway, why are you up? Isn't it like, four in the morning there?" She signed off with a wink before he could get his words out.

~

"This is good news, people," she said, after she didn't get response she was expecting. She glanced down at Dawes to see that he was as confused as they were. "We're in a state of emergency. So we have an additional four units of UNPF on the way. Today. Basically, we're doubling our numbers."

The looks that glanced back up her, the downturned eyes suddenly showing some hope, filled her heart with warmth. It was a minor victory, tiny in fact, but she had made their lives better. This went some of the way toward making up the guilt she felt for the team members she'd lost. Even though she had been assured that it was just a case of bad timing and being in the wrong place, she would always blame herself.

Her team went out onto the landings to their tasks, enthused and not in the mood to take any shit from the prisoners hell-bent on giving them another day of pain.

"Ma'am," Dawes said from a desk behind her. "Comm for you." She frowned, unsure why the unit comm would be used instead of her personal set.

"Brandt here," she said, picking up the headset to hold it to one ear.

"Brandt, Commander Franks," came the gruff voice. "I'm sending Lieutenant Commander Bowen to your location. When he arrives, consider yourself relieved."

Her heart, slightly lifted by the results of her meddling, dropped.

"Sir, might I ask the reason for my dismi—"

"No, you may not. You will be escorted here. Franks out."

"Shit," Brandt said, drawing out the word and seeing a confused and concerned ensign staring at her like a puppy. "You're getting a new boss," she told him.

"When?" A buzzer sounded, warning that the main airlocked doors to the unit were opening.

"Now, I guess."

The replacement officer seemed nice enough, asking for Dawes to give him a run-down of the unit and wishing Brandt luck. She left, flanked by the two quiet UNPF seamen. Neither of them said a word as they traveled back to the hub and to Franks's office door.

~

"Ah, Lieutenant Commander Brandt," Franks said with a smile that made her instantly suspicious. She walked inside, still wearing her armor but with her helmet clipped to her waist. "These people are from UNID, and they'd like to talk to you."

The reason for his smile suddenly became obvious to her. He thought she was in serious trouble if the UNID came calling. She stepped inside to see Torres and a younger woman with almost unnaturally smooth brown skin wearing the two vertical gold stars of a Lieutenant on her right shoulder. Torres gave her a look as though it was the first time they had met, so she played along.

"How can I help you?"

"We need to debrief you further regarding the matter prior to your court-martial," Torres said stiffly. Behind him Franks smiled cruelly.

"Not a problem," she responded as she looked to Franks. "If you have no objection, sir?"

"No, none at all, goodbye Lieutenant Commander."

~

"Couldn't keep your head down if you tried, could you?" Torres said tiredly as soon as they were in an elevator alone.

"Me?" she asked innocently.

"You think using your chip wouldn't leave a trace? You think it wouldn't actually cause a red flag that would fetch me a comm call from the UNID director in the middle of the night? I specifically told you: *low profile.*"

"Oh…"

"Yeah, *oh*," he said. "Brandt, this is Eze." He pronounced it as *Ay-zay* and the young woman smiled at her and offered a hand.

"Amare," she said in a rich East African-edged accent, giving her first name. "It's an honor to meet you." Her voice was cultured and British to Brandt's ear, like she had lived on two different continents in her youth. "Call me Viper." Her CP special operations callsign acted as a kind of resume.

"Likewise," Brandt said. "Grip." She turned back to Torres, and couldn't keep the suspicion from her voice. "So what now?"

"Not here," he told her as they walked into her accommodation. "Personal gear only. Travel light and leave the armor."

Shit, Brandt thought to herself. *I've really screwed up this time. Why didn't I just leave it alone?*

She stuffed the few items of clothing and belongings into her bag, which she zipped down to make it smaller. Fully loaded there was no way she could carry it without the powered armor she had just struggled out of. She didn't ask any more questions and followed meekly behind Torres as they left the accommodation compound. In the elevator leading back toward the main exit of the complex, Torres and Eze carefully removed and folded their uniform jackets to reveal black tactical trousers and an over-shoulder harness. The jackets went into the small bag that Eze carried and civilian coats came out to replace them. Torres wore the same weathered leather jacket he had on when they met a few nights previously, and Eze sported a collarless shell jacket. Both allowed them easy access to the rigs under their arms, which now carried two pistols identical to the one used in the bar.

Brandt opened her mouth to speak but Torres reiterated his earlier words.

"Not here," he said again, passing her another pistol. She checked it and tucked it into the back of her waistband. "Go covert and follow my lead."

CHAPTER 17

Joint UNID/Hyper Research Facility, Lunar Surface

It had taken them almost an hour to reach their destination via the transit network, the subterranean trains hurtling along the tunnels at impossible speeds. As soon as they had reached the promenade, Eze had melted away. Only flashes of her rich skin flashed in and out of focus in the sparse crowds. Brandt walked beside Torres, who was blending in. His manner prompted her to adapt her mannerisms and be ultra-alert while feigning the boredom and disinterest of commuters galaxy-wide. She sat, her bag next to her and her eyes seemingly looking out of the window, but in truth she was using the reflection of the lighted interior to see the entrance to the train car she was in. Torres was sitting just inside her field of vision, looking like he was exhausted, as his head lolled gently with the soft movement of the missile they were riding.

Eze was nowhere to be seen, but Brandt had seen enough of her to guess that this was one of her born specialisms. She guessed that the lieutenant would be somewhere close by and could probably give a description and threat assessment of most people in the car.

The train slowed, and the lights were raised as it approached another station. Brandt saw Torres stir and stretch as though getting ready to disembark. She readied the straps of her bag and shifted in her seat, not moving much but enough to appear as though she was preparing to leave.

She let Torres move first, dropping into line three people behind him as she stepped down to the platform and followed him. She weaved between people, taking the moving staircase upward where the air grew thicker and warmer. The first thing she noticed when she reached surface level was the increased presence of UNPF troops in armor, in addition to the uniformed security guards. The curious addition, one that she hadn't seen deployed in civilian areas before, were the larger mech suits with bigger weaponry on show. Standing at double the height of the armored troops, who themselves were uncharacteristically armed with carbines and pistols, the mech army was a looming show of force. She couldn't figure out why.

She followed Torres, still having no glimpse of Eze, and found herself going to what looked like a closed terminal. Torres looked around, nodding to her, and swiped his left forearm over the door, which popped open. He held it for her, shutting it behind them.

"What about Eze?"

"She'll follow, let's go," he said as he pointed her toward a small train with a single car. They climbed inside and it set off immediately.

"What the hell is going on?" she asked. "Why are there mech-rigs on patrol in Grand Central?"

"Your request worked," he said almost angrily, "and five units landed this morning, fully equipped. Two are dealing with the penal facility, two have bolstered the CTSC patrols and one is in reserve, dotted all over the place."

"My request?"

"Come on," he said. "Your fingerprints are all over it. Why couldn't you just do what we asked? We have to accelerate our timeline now."

"Why? What timeline? What's going on?"

"We're leaving the Moon," he answered, taking a deep breath and letting it out slowly. "I'm sorry, it's not entirely your fault." Brandt looked at him, waiting for an explanation. "The communique to Earth was sent to the Combined Territories, not the UN in America…"

"And?"

"And it had a UNID flag on it, so everyone paid close attention. That got some people checking on what other territories were here and what they were doing. Get it?"

"Oh, so… what?"

"So, we have potentially hostile UNID operatives from other territories here looking for answers. They've probably flagged us and seen that our transport manifests are interwoven with Hyper's. That or else they've noticed that half of our personnel are hidden among other deployment lists or else are just plain old missing. Everything we are doing here is covert, and it smacks of under the table dealing if you look at it closely. Those operatives sent here work for territories that are actively trying to steal tech advances and are funding global terrorism. We don't know how high up their influence goes, whether it's the work of individuals or entire territories, so we're moving off ahead of schedule. So in one way, you get your wish."

"Crap. Kyle, I'm sorry," Brandt said. "I didn't mean to…"

"I know," he said tiredly. "It's not really your fault, you're just a very small part of the problem. In one way, at least they came in force and didn't just send their own SpecOps after us quietly."

The train slowed and stopped. Torres's face relaxed—they had reached safety.

"Come see the Aladdin's cave," he told her, "and prepare to meet an old friend. Or two."

Brandt walked through the security checkpoint, allowing her arm to be scanned so the shield blocking the inner entrance could be dropped. Once she had walked through, it powered up again behind her.

"Welcome to the next level," Torres said. All the stress of their vulnerability had been seemingly forgotten as he waved forward a young man in uniform to take her bag. "We have the new armor, which you've already used, but we also have new weaponry. Check the pistol I gave you."

She did, drawing it from behind her back and inspecting it.

"See the port ahead of the barrel? Where the mag would go in a USP?"

She nodded.

He tossed her a small battery unit and showed her with his own gun how it fitted.

"Armor piercing like you've never known. No plate on Earth, or up here for that matter, will stand up to one of these."

"How does it work?" she asked, holding the pistol with a new-found wariness.

"It adds a singularity charge to each projectile, kind of like a secondary power source but it also gives it a sort of field. I'm not one hundred percent on the science, obviously, but I can vouch for it working. We have the same set-up with the new carbines and rifles, too."

Brandt followed him into a room where lines of small, white-bodied guns adorned the walls. Racks of pistols sat below the examples of longer rifles and heavy support guns on display.

Brandt gawped as she passed through the room and into the next, again using her implanted chip as her access card. More people occupied this room, some of them stopping to look up at who had walked in, before putting their heads down again.

"This is amazing," she said, seeing the ranks of new armor standing on charging platforms.

Torres laughed.

"Hold that thought," he told her, turning to face her and wearing a look of intense seriousness. "You wanted in? Like, all the way in? This is it. Choose now. Are you in or—"

"I'm in," Brandt said quickly.

Torres eyed her, a smile spreading slowly across his face. "Good, because this next shit will blow your mind."

~

"Jamie?" Brandt said. She stared open-mouthed at the scientist explaining something to a man with his back to her.

"Les," he said with evident pleasure. "Glad you made it."

"I... what are... Okay, *someone* start from the beginning here?"

"Doctor Paterson here is one of the leads on the developmental project we are here for," Torres said.

"*Doctor* Paterson?" she asked.

"Yeah, sorry I didn't keep in touch, *Commander*..."

Fair point, she thought, letting her demotion slip her mind for a moment.

"So, you're a weapons designer now?"

"Hell, no," Paterson said. "That's our private friends who do that. No, I'm more of the Einstein-Rosen type and less of the *pew-pew-pew.*"

Her confused look made him sigh with disappointment. "An Einstei—"

"I know what a wormhole is, dumbass," she said, cutting him off. "The theoretical ability to fold space-time to connect two points of any distance together." Paterson smiled at her, making her feel like she was a show-off but still dumb as a lump of moonrock by comparison. Just like he always used to.

"Theoretical?"

Brandt's eyes went wide, and her open mouth slowly formed the shape to utter words.

"No fuc—"

"Yep," he said before she cursed the entire lab to the ground. "But don't just take my word for it."

Brandt was so wrapped up in the revelations that she didn't notice the man Paterson had been speaking to when she entered. He slipped away quietly, moving so smoothly that it was almost unnatural. He watched from the shadows of one corner as Paterson set up the experiment for her.

"We've been developing a thing called the Fold Drive," he told her. "It has the ability to move things through space without it actually physically occupying that space. In effect, things go from one place to the other in an instant. Well, depending on the distances involved, but that's not been tested yet." He led her to one end of the room to a tall, shielded dome about the size of two people.

"Is this... Is this a shield unit? This small?"

Paterson looked at Torres with annoyance. "You haven't even showed her *that* yet?"

"Sorry, Brandt," Torres said. "We have some personal shield emitters now. That tech's been around for a couple of years now."

Brandt's mind spun but Paterson got her attention again. "See how there's nothing inside?" She nodded. "Good, go over to that one and see that it's empty too." She did as she was told, walking across the lab to the identical shield dome and turning back to nod at him like he was about to perform a magic trick. He looked around, finding a tray of coffee cups and a sugar pot and deactivated the dome before putting it inside. He tapped at a control panel and the dome buzzed back into life.

"Okay then," he muttered to himself, "Initializing in four, three, two, one..."

Light flashed inside the dome. It wasn't a searing, blinding light but one that made her eyes react with an involuntary blink to the simple pop it gave off. When she blinked the tray of cups had gone. She turned slowly to look inside the dome she was standing by and saw the tray beside her.

"Ho-ly shiii-it," she said.

"I know, right?" Paterson said with barely disguised glee, like he was a drunken frat boy having just discovered the ancient art of beer pong.

"So, it's a teleporter?" she asked.

"No," Paterson said, his face registering something bordering on disgust. "That's a *completely* different kind of science."

"Does it work with people?"

"Ah," Paterson said, his glee diminishing instantly. "Not yet. Organic material has a nasty habit of, um, *exploding* a little bit?" He held his forefinger and thumb a short distance apart, as though the concept of exploding was one that could be mitigated by the use of a sliding scale of severity. Her eyes showed that she wasn't too impressed with the concept and he shrugged.

"That's only if it's exposed," he explained. "The theory is that inside armor it would work."

"The theory?"

"Worked with mice inside a sealed box," he said weakly, his shoulders up around his ears.

"So, it'll work with a person inside a suit?" she asked.

"In theory," Torres said to cut in, "but that isn't the main event, is it?"

"What? Oh no, we've fitted this to a prototype ship."

Brandt shook her head, thinking that she wouldn't be able to take the information overload she was experiencing. Everything was being turned on its head, from realizing that the armor she had spent years trusting her life to was vulnerable to a goddamned hand cannon, to the fact that she no longer, in theory, had to walk from one side of the planet to another.

"Come see it," Torres said, leading the way up some steps to a viewing platform.

The *Bōken-sha Ichi*, or Explorer One, was the culmination of almost nine years of engineering expertise. The constant testing and redesigning of prototypes until a design won through for further development. It was, just as most of the tech Brandt had walked by, like nothing she had ever seen. No doubt it would filter down to the rest of the population in about two decades, but the cutting edge of design existed primarily in the realms of private money and secret projects.

The sleek lines of the elongated transport mesmerized her, the way it flowed from the sharply pointed nose to the upward sweeping curves of the delta wing design that culminated in an array of quad engines protruding out of the back.

The only disruption to that sleekness was the bulbous extensions of gunner's compartments fore and aft where quad chain gun barrels protruded so menacingly that it looked both reassuring and terrifying all at once.

Her eyebrows met as she considered this, trying to figure out where the large access would be, given the sheer size of the ship. She saw just ahead of the rear landing struts a long ramp leading down to the hangar deck like it was a giant metal marsupial. The main body of the ship stretched ahead of this with no portholes visible. Ending back at the nose, shaped like a missile, she saw not one straight line on the prototype craft, which looked as though it had been shaped from water and not constructed of different pieces of alloy.

"Wow," she said, grossly underselling what she saw. This was too weak a word to do the sight justice.

"Wow is about right," Paterson told her. "She's fitted with four singularity drives—the ones that power whole cities—and she can make Mars in a month under normal power."

"Normal power?" Brandt asked.

"There's a fifth singularity source up front underneath the cockpit that powers the shield array and the Fold Drive emitter." He pointed to the long protrusion in front of the nose where it stuck out like a swordfish.

"Fold Drive emitter?"

"Yeah, it projects the specific intensity and frequency of electromagnetic field to penetrate space-time. It's like a kind of... *space drill*, and it goes out just ahead of the shielding to protect everyone and everything inside."

"But does that protect against… whatever it is that turns organic material inside out?"

"So long as the shielding stays in place, yes. That's why I've linked them to the same power source. Any failure of power to the shields will automatically cut the Fold Drive before that, so we'd effectively reappear in normal space-time before our shielding fell and we turned into liquid."

"Reassuring," she commented. "So have you tested it yet?"

"No," he answered, still grinning like an idiot, "but we might on the way to Mars."

"Why Mars?" she asked, turning to Torres.

"We have another lab there," he said, earning a confused look from Paterson this time too. He said no more on the matter. "We need to prep for departure. Brandt? A word?" She stepped to one side as the others melted away.

"Listen, I know this has all got pretty weird today, but…"

"Weird? I'll say."

"Yeah," Torres said. "Well it's about to get a little weirder."

"How?"

"Remember the last time we were all here?" he asked. Brandt said nothing.

"Well… well it's a full reunion, if you catch my drift." She didn't. She *couldn't*. He was forced to say it outright.

"Jake…" He paused as she gasped quietly and stared at him with glistening eyes. "Jake didn't technically die back then."

She knew it. Suddenly her vivid memory of the transport ride back down to Earth filled her mind. Showing her an image of Horne and his two goons guarding those black crates, which came back with a clarity she didn't expect.

"They've got people in there," she said to her friends. *She had opened a private channel to their suit designations and spoke privately thanks to the sealed armor.* *"Injured people. That was a resuscitation they just did."*

It was. It must have been. It had been a resuscitation and it was Jake being kept alive.

"I want to see him. Is he here? Now? Where is he?"

"It's not that simple," Torres said, both hands up to try and calm her growing stress.

"What do you mean it's not—"

"Precisely what he says." A voice with a metallic quality spoke from the shadows behind Torres.

She stared. It wasn't that dark there but whoever had spoken had been so utterly still that she doubted any human being could have maintained cover so effectively. A dark, black-gloved hand rested on Torres's shoulder as the figure stepped forward.

"It's okay, Kyle," the voice said. "I will explain all I can."

Torres nodded, looked once more at Brandt and walked away. She looked at the shadowy figure. The height, the pattern and softness of his voice, all of it pointed to a name on the tip of her tongue.

"Jake?" she whispered, barely able to control her breathing.

"In a way. I am Specter. This is what remains of Jake Santana's body," the voice said. "But I'm... I'm not completely him and he isn't completely me. It's like living with someone else's memories and emotions inside me. I was... *reborn* in a sense and have had to learn many things since I had new arms and new legs and could see again. I had to learn how to speak, to walk, and many other things." He stepped forward, revealing the green glow of his artificial eyes and then the sleek, black-clad body beneath.

Very faint sounds of machine components reached her ears, but she couldn't understand in that moment what caused them. She looked into his scarred face and tried to speak, to say something that would bring him back to her.

"Jake…" was all she could whisper again.

"Specter," he answered softly. "You'll get used to it in time."

"No," she said, reaching for her forearm and realizing she didn't have her comm device strapped to her, nor did she have her datapad as it was in her bag in another part of the facility. She wanted to show him the picture she still kept on her devices. Wanted to remind him that they had been a team, that the three of them were back together no matter how much they had all changed. He gave her a sad smile, just like he used to—like Jake used to—and turned to walk away.

Brandt stood glued to the spot, unable to move or think, only able to repeat one word to herself in a whisper.

"Jake."

An angry shout from the next room cut through her stupor, and she jogged to catch up with Torres. He flicked through an incoming comm on his wrist screen.

"We're blown," he said. "UN East and Africa have flashed an alert message; we're officially persons of interest in espionage and terrorism."

"Bastards," Brandt said. She had to admit, though, that was the best way to bring anyone down and not have a word they said listened to.

"It's everyone on our manifest," he said. "UNID and Hyper. This intelligence had to come from inside, for God's sake."

"So, what do we do?"

Torres never had the chance to answer before his comm chirped and blinked again.

CHAPTER 18

Lunar Grand Central Train Station

"Viper to Taco," Amare Eze said.

Fourteen miles away in the reinforced bunker laboratory

Torres's mouth formed a tight line. He hated the callsign they had given him when he first got selected for the CP teams, but when they stuck, they stuck for life.

He had been called so because he was still small back then and one of the training staff said he was snack-sized. In their defense they didn't know his surname, and if they had, they might not have made the connection to the admiral with the same name. They would have been even less likely to have guessed that she had a son in the service about his age. So the callsign he hated became a part of him that he'd lived with for too long.

"Torres here. Go ahead, Viper," he answered into his comm, snapping his fingers for everyone around him to shut the hell up and switch on.

"We have movement on the main promenade above Lunar Grand Central train station. UNPF from the Eastern and African territories, by the look of them, are clearing out all civilian personnel and shutting down all trains in and out.

They are currently arguing with what looks like the senior guy from the private security forces."

"Are you compromised?" he asked the comm. This question made those within earshot perk up and look more alive than they had a moment before.

"Negative," Eze replied. "I am in a service entrance near to our cache. I am going for my armor, but I don't know if I can make extraction."

"Stand down, Viper," Torres said with authority, "There's an alert out for all of us for global terrorism. Return to base immediately. Do not get compromised and do not get captured, do you copy?"

A pause. Torres cursed himself for losing her before the mission had started. He knew she would get captured eventually, and that the UNID would retrieve her quietly, but she would be stranded and she would miss the mission that she desperately wanted to be on. He wanted her to be there.

"Copy," she said softly, "but I need my armor to RTB. Out."

~

"Dammit," Torres said angrily. He knew her. He knew that she intended to disobey almost everything he just said to her, before turning to the assembled people milling about the labs. He looked around them, seeing too many to address in one go. He hit a series of icons on his wrist screen.

"Lockdown," his voice boomed out of the speakers in every part of the lab. "Lockdown. All personnel assigned to the *Ichi* board immediately and prepare for take-off. All combat personnel, form on me in zone one. Torres out."

Movement exploded in the labs, as everyone bust a gut to be where they needed to be with what they needed to have in seconds. Brandt ran up to Torres.

"Where do you need me?" she asked.

"With me, Commander," he said, setting off for the doorway into zone two at a dead run. He stopped in front of the ranks of new armor suits, their names stamped on the right chest and on the back of the helmets.

Torres stopped in front of one and attached his wrist comm to the suit and stepped back as it split open like a puzzle. He turned around, threw off his jacket and dropped his new pistol onto a table. "Your rank is reinstated. So is my promotion to Commander."

He backed in and stood still as the armor closed up again around him. As the visor mirrored over the suit came to life, he turned to look at Brandt. She had retrieved her own wrist unit from her bag and fixed it to the suit marked 'BRANDT – CMDR'. She stripped off her jacket and put her pistol next to his, turned and backed into her armor.

She felt her limbs and torso reassuringly squeezed as the plates locked together and sealed, then her hair got caught as the helmet hinged closed. She gritted her teeth and moved her head to rip free the handful of painful strands pinched in the metal. The visor flash to life as the HUD blinked on. Dozens of tiny symbols ranged around her field of vision. The outlines of other soldiers and scientists locked red for a fraction of a second and their details blinked beside them, ready for her to ring up the file if she chose to. She didn't look at them. Instead, she stepped down from the platform with a light metallic clang to pick up the weapon and hold it against her right thigh. It mag-locked in an instant, and she let go of the pistol's grip to ensure it stayed there, before grasping it again and feeling it come immediately loose in her gauntlet. She mag-locked it again and looked to her right.

Torres stood taller than her, his chest bearing the same rank code as hers. He appeared hulking but still mobile in his armor, and his voice came out of the speakers on his suit and into the audio receptors of her own.

"Follow me," he said, running toward the first zone nearest the entrance where the racks of weapons were.

"Chief, you good here?" he barked at the back of a man who was organizing soldiers into defensive positions. The man spun, his armor a slightly darker shade of gray than her own, and she read the name stenciled on his chest high up on the right. *Horne.*

Too much of a coincidence, she thought.

"I got this," he said. "You going after your team member?"

"Yes," Torres said. "Nobody in or out, unless it is us, got that?"

"Got it," Horne said, glancing at Brandt and taking her armored form in for the first time.

And he called me Chief to try and appease me, she thought.

Torres walked to a weapons rack and took two small carbines, both much lighter and shorter than the bulky service rifles they knew intimately.

"Seventy round mag," he said as he took one and fitted it to the gun in front of her. It ran in a long curve from the rear stock, under the trigger guard and to the foregrip.

"Singularity charge." He held one up to her and showed her how that fitted into the hollow section ahead of the foregrip. "Safety, sub or supersonic." He pointed to two switches, one to activate the bang-bang function and one to choose the speed of those bangs. He passed her three spare magazines, which she slotted into the clips on her chest, and added an extra two for the pistol to her left thigh.

"What about the singularity thing?" she asked.

"Just don't lose it," he told her. "Those things are good for about eighty thousand rounds. One more thing," he said as he reached for a pair of large, flat items about the same size of the discus but heavier. He slapped one against the small of her back where it stuck and held his up before her.

"Mobile cover," he said, slapping it down to the deck where the top snapped open in two half circles and a shaft of shimmering blue light appeared upward. The light spread to about the height of their suits and twice the width. He took another and fixed it to his back.

"If you think you need to use it," he told her, "then it should already be on the deck."

Her head spun even more.

Where the hell has all this tech come from? she thought. *Shield emitters are the size of apartments, so how the hell is this possible? No time,* she interrupted herself. *Work first, ask later.*

As if he read her thoughts, Torres's voice sounded inside her helmet on the private channel he had opened up.

"I'll explain later," he said. "Right now I need you on my six."

"Wait. Aren't we going to bring anything heavier? I mean, they've got battle mechs and we're using six-millimeter?"

Torres turned to face her. Inside his own helmet she knew he was smiling. "We have *armor-piercing* six-millimeter. Trust me."

They took the train module back toward the main station, hoping they weren't too late to get their stranded operator out of there before all hell broke loose.

Neither of them wanted a firefight, especially not against UNPF troops who were almost certainly being given corrupt orders to carry out and not understanding the first thing about them, but needs must. In this case, those needs were of the few over the many. Those few had a mission to undertake that could change the course of humanity and advance them beyond their wildest dreams.

Beyond their solar system.

~

Viper, as she called herself, had slipped into the service areas away from the main public sections of the train station and its platforms. They had a secret cache there, where Eze had left her armor and carbine in an innocuous-looking storage cupboard which was reinforced and only opened for a UNID biochip. The cupboard, for as long as anyone working there could recall, had been marked as out of order following some kind of contaminant leak. That was enough to ensure that the highly irregular remained hidden in plain, public sight as was the way of the Intelligence Directorate.

She stepped inside her armor, quietly retrieved her weapons and stepped out of the cupboard to make her way toward the single train tunnel that led back to the Hyper lab. She almost made it, utilizing the target recognition software to its full effect, until a keen-eyed seaman, all of nineteen years old by the high-pitched tone of his voice, yelled a challenge in Arabic from behind her.

She stopped, seeing the words translated onto her HUD: "Halt. Identify yourself."

She stopped, turning to face him and recognizing the body language of a double-take. As one of the few places left on Earth to still discriminate with such things, Eze knew that most of the Arab parts of the Eastern territory still forbade women to serve in the UNPF. The sight of a female in armor was nothing new elsewhere, but this unit clearly had no females on station.

Shit, she thought sourly. *Think.*

175

She held up her left hand to greet the young solider as she whipped the pistol off her thigh with her right hand and drilled three rounds into the center of his chest plate. She swept the carbine one-handed to where her HUD showed two more armored troops on the other side of a wall. As the boy dropped to his knees and pitched forward onto his faceplate, the two other soldiers started toward the body. They were unaware of the danger as they ran directly into a hail of supersonic bullets that tore through their suits. Shouts rang out; the death of three soldiers set alarm bells ringing inside every UNPF helmet there.

Eze turned and ran to the tunnel entrance as the first few bullets pinged harmlessly off of her armor, just as her HUD registered two outlines of armored troops who flashed red, then turned gold and registered on her display as her allies. An icon flashed low under her left eye, which she fixed in a split-second to join the active comm channel open between their suits.

"Am I glad to see you..." she said as the train stopped and the door hissed open. An impact knocked her off her feet as a heavy round ricocheted off the back of her right shoulder before she could step forward. The heavy bullet, a 12mm, was not alone. The first shot missed them, having glanced off the armor of Eze, but the twenty or so friends that followed it ploughed straight into the side of the train and made a noise like tortured metal being killed with electricity and submerged in water.

The hissing and fizzing spoke of something very wrong, but the more immediate concern was the source of the heavy weaponry still incoming. As they turned, their HUDs recognized the outline of a battle mech. Standing like a giant bipedal frog, the thing's arms jutted forward and pumped round after round of heavy ammo into their position. The soldiers took cover, cowering out of sight and feeling grateful that the armor of these low-rent units would not have been updated with the new battlefield recognition software yet.

"We're pinned down," Torres said in a normal voice. It was one of the benefits of fighting inside sealed armor with an open comm link. Brandt readied her weapon and took the disc from her back.

"Toss yours out," she said. "Give me ten meters."

Torres hesitated only marginally but reached behind himself and lobbed the flat device out into the open arena ahead of them. Brandt ran to it, sliding in on her knees as she lobbed her own mobile cover shield another ten meters ahead. Just as the grunt driving the battle mech reacted to where she was, she was up and running again, sprinting toward the device she had just thrown before the shield had chance to emerge and take shape.

Time seemed to slow as both arm cannons swung toward her on rapid-reacting hydraulics. The mech stepped its left leg back to angle the guns down better. It was a race to see whether the shield would be up by the time she got there or whether the bullets would start to fly and pin her to the deck. They could penetrate her armor and crush her under the weight of the incoming projectiles. She saw muzzle flashes from both attacking arms as she threw herself into a roll, coming up just in time to see the pinprick of black in her vision as a bullet travelled directly toward her. The growing panel of light blue energy rose ahead of it, flashing brightly as the impact dissipated its kinetic energy against the shield. Brandt crashed into it and saw the base unit connect to her HUD and give a readout of sixty-seven percent.

Jesus, her brain yelled at her, *can't stay here!*

Her mind knew this, but her body wasn't willing to play ball. She forced herself to move, to spin out of the cover before it faltered and left her exposed. She did so a second ahead of the heavy guns, which were only ten feet away from her. She rose, safety off and finger curling around the trigger as the gun vibrated and chattered away in her hands. She kept the pressure on, walking the almost constant stream of bullets into the arms of the mech until they stopped firing. When they did stop, and the driver realized what danger he was now in, he drove the big rig straight at her to try and mow her down.

Brandt rolled to the side, unclipping a new magazine from her chest and fitting it to the unfamiliar gun with more intuitive ease than she expected. She then flicked back the short pull of the charging handle, and swung the barrel to point directly up under the cockpit.

She let it rip, emptying the entire magazine into the belly of the mech, and watched in awe as the rounds began to tear out of the top, passing through the driver on their way. The battle mech fell backward, the rig mimicking the dying movements of the suited human at the controls and landed with a massive clang.

Brandt reloaded. Only then was she aware of the dozens of other red outlines pinging up on her HUD as the incoming rounds bounced off her armor. The sound of Torres's voice came back to her then.

"Brandt? You crazy bitch—the *hell* are you doing?"

She ducked back behind the mobile cover and answered him, seeing the splatter of light on the shield as bullets struck it. The readout stayed steady, barely noticing the low-velocity rounds.

"What does it look like? Stopping the goddamned battle mech!"

"Well, get your ass back here. The train is toast and we need another way back."

Brandt thought about it, glancing down to see her cover drop another one percent as an insane idea crossed her mind.

"Is there an emergency airlock on this level?" she asked.

"Yes…" Torres answered. She could tell he didn't like where this was going.

"How far to the lab? Three miles?"

"Oh no," Torres said, immediately. "No fucking way. Dammit, Brandt… *you're insane!*"

"Eze, where's the airlock?" she asked. She popped up from her cover to fire six rapid bursts at a squad who had tried to flank her, using a thin wall as cover.

"Fifty-eight meters behind us," Eze answered after a quick check through her suit's software.

"Go," Brandt told them.

"Wait one," Torres cut in. "Okay, done. Moving." Brand tried to think what had caused his short delay, but her HUD showed a flashing display saying 'armed' above the shield percentage.

"You might want to move, Commander," Torres told her.

She turned, running hard away from the shield about to detonate. They ran, reaching the emergency airlock and taking up defensive positions as Eze overrode the security protocols to activate it. As soon as the first door rolled to one side to open, another flurry of heavy rounds found their mark and slammed Eze into the doorframe. She was left unmoving on the deck. Brandt started to fire bursts into the battle mech, the lead one of three now in sight, but her carbine couldn't hope to match the destructive power of six heavy guns at that distance. She turned to Torres, who seemed to understand their situation just as quickly.

"Torres to base," he said with a heavy tone of regret. "I don't think we're going to make it back. Initiate take-off sequence and be ready to go without us—don't let that ship be captured."

CHAPTER 19

UNID/Hyper Base, Eight Miles from Grand Central

"Dammit, Brandt... *you're insane!*" Specter heard over the radio channel he had infiltrated.

His limited knowledge of the base had been enough to know that the train was their only way in or out via the main lunar transit system. If that train was damaged, the three of them would be fighting their way back against impossible odds. Two entire units against three soldiers, regardless of how well they were trained and whether they had a technological advantage, just wouldn't cut it. He would even up those odds. Seeing as he didn't really answer to anyone there, he took the initiative.

Walking straight up to his unique matte black armor with additional interfaces and faster prototype servos to make the suit move faster, he stepped inside and interfaced with the HUD wirelessly. The suit moved as fast as his biomechanical limbs did, thanks to the faster tech and direct neural interface linked to the existing tech they had installed in his body over the years. He ran to the weapons racks, taking two pistols and spare magazines, as well as the new battle rifle chambered in the heavier 12mm caliber.

"The hell are you going with that?" someone asked from behind him.

"Out," he said to the man wearing the armor labeled 'Horne'. He opened the shield entrance with visual interface and stepped through it.

"There's no train here, dumbass," he was told. He smiled to himself and set off jogging along the tunnel, gathering momentum quickly until his arms and legs whipped back and forth so fast that his movement became a blur. It was a strange, alien sensation to be running so fast and not actually be moving his own body; he was simply activating the mechanical additions to his torso. It was more like he was driving his exoskeleton as opposed to actually running. The end result with the uprated armor was a sprint that reached over sixty miles per hour on the smooth rock floor carved out by the advanced mining tools brought up to the Moon's surface so long ago.

"Screw him," Horne said as he turned back to the mix of UNID and Hyper soldiers. "You heard the man, move!"

Their defenses were abandoned and as the big prototype vessel was boarded by a mass of people. Horne kept the soldiers back, forming a loose half circle facing away from the ship in case any of their former friends came to prevent their escape. It was unfortunate for him that people, most likely decent, honest people as he had been, were now under orders to try to kill or capture him. He didn't envy them their task, but neither did he feel so much empathy that he would allow either option to happen. He had his mission, and he would achieve it.

~

"Cover!" Torres said over their channel, timing the passing of the big battle mechs just right and detonating the mobile shield cover.

It blew right between the leading pair of them, taking off the nearest legs of each in an instant and toppling them so that their cockpits—their heads—clanged massively off one another as they fell. They formed a new barrier as they went down, spreading out the attacking troops. This wasn't to their benefit. The flow of attackers, wary after the armor they had trusted in proved to be as useful as wearing wet paper towels, came quickly on their right flank as Brandt's firing stopped.

"Last mag," she said as she slapped it in and whipped back the charging handle. She spun to fire concentrated bursts at the threatening approach.

"Same," Torres answered with the slightest hint of stress in his voice. "Eze, you still with us?"

Eze groaned groggily over the channel. She was alive but clearly she wasn't much good to them. They didn't know if her armor had been penetrated or whether she was banged up inside. She could have a malfunction in the software or the hardware for all they knew, but they did know only the two of them were effective at that moment.

"Covering fire," Torres instructed, waiting for Brandt to switch and fire longer bursts at targets on all approaches. He slipped from cover, hearing the booming reports of the big guns on the mechs as he sprinted and dropped to slide to the now-open inner door of the airlock. Eze was moving unnaturally, trying to sit up but jerking like a landed fish.

"Need to reboot," she said with a gasp. She was out of breath as her suit was forcing her to move and not the other way around. Torres reassured her that she was going to be fine, spinning her over to see the three dents and a long score mark on her back and right shoulder where the bullets had hit her but not penetrated the suit.

He accessed her program wirelessly using his own operating system. As quickly as he could, Torres forced her suit to shut down and cancelled all of the error messages and warnings that flashed up on his display. The jerking armor powered down, sinking into relaxation as Eze lay flat on her back, trapped inside the alloy can.

She forced herself to breathe slowly and steadily, not wanting to use up all of the remaining air stored inside. The environmental scrubbers were offline along with everything else. Her visor, usually a riot of colored displays and icons, was clear and she could see the mirrored visor of Torres, who was stripping the spare magazines from her chest.

"Here," she heard him shout. She watched him disappear from her small, paralyzed window of vision. He came back without the two magazines he had taken from her and tapped at his forearm unit. Her visor went black, powering up as a progress bar appeared before her eyes. She felt the sudden coolness of the suit's air recycling and her movements again began to correspond to the articulation of her armor. The message, 'Reboot complete; send error report to UNID?' came up before her. She raised a hand and tapped at the empty air above her to hit the option to agree. Torres had gone again, leaving her with a full weapon and one replacement magazine. She rose to a crouch to get back into the fight.

"Left flank," Brandt warned.

Torres had seen them, and waited for them to break cover to cross the open ground in the public place that was never designed as a battlefield. His carbine juddered intensely in his hands as the squad ran for his position.

"Center," Eze snapped, taking cover and firing bursts at one of the remaining mechs advancing on them. The unit that they faced must have been fully equipped to have so many heavy units in play;

it was almost as though someone giving their orders expected them to be facing a firefight against superior technology. The three soldiers switched their aim, their combined bullets drilling into the alloy beast until the penetrating rounds hit something vital. Up close, Brandt had carved through one of them, but she had fired on full-auto from only a few meters away. At the range they were engaging, a lot of the rounds were being absorbed or deflected by the thicker armor.

"We need to go. Now," Brandt said.

"No," Torres snapped back as he fired. "We need to hold them off for as long as possible so that the ship can get clear."

Brandt wanted to argue. Wanted to rage at him and tell him that they had to get back to the ship, that they *were* the mission's best chance of success and that they shouldn't waste their lives in a delaying action.

She aimed her carbine at the nearest mech, squeezing off shots aimed at the cockpit to try to neutralize the pilot. As she fired, the mech rocked from three impacts coming from its right. Brandt scanned to her left, seeing another armored soldier emerging from the tunnel entrance ahead of their destroyed train, firing a rifle. She could see the faint blue whispers the bullets left, like an echo of their energy lingering in the air, and heard the electric buzz of their passage ending in the huge impacts striking the mech. It went down after five shots, the last of which passed through in a straight line to decapitate two soldiers taking cover on the far side of it.

"Move to this exit," a voice said over their comm link. It had that same twang to it, that hint of synthesized words like an accent long faded. It had a faded accent too—that Latin Californian edge that she had never forgotten.

"Negative, Jake," she said, forgetting herself in the heat of battle. "Too confined. Form on us. We're going outside."

The comm channel was silent for a moment. "Understood," came the reply.

"Eze, how are we looking on that airlock?" Torres barked.

"Good to go," she told him, reloading her last magazine and snapping back the handle to rattle off longer bursts before she moved.

Torres waited a heartbeat as they both watched Jake —*Specter*— running toward them at an impossible speed. Brandt sprinted the short distance back, reaching the entrance of the airlock and turning to add her gun to the fight. Specter ran past Torres and slowed to turn and offer support. Torres emptied his magazine as Specter raised the battle rifle. Smaller bullets pinged and whined off his armor as he moved. Just as Torres made it to his feet and started to move, a great shadow descended as a squad of armored soldiers dropped from the level above directly behind him. One tripped him, sending him sprawling out and losing his gun as it skittered ahead of him out of reach. He spun onto his back, his right hand snatching at the pistol grip of the gun on his right thigh. But an armored boot, heavier and broader than their own suits, stamped to pin him down. A squad support weapon was pointed at his chest at point blank range.

He froze, knowing that the weapon would carve through him at point blank range to tear through armor, flesh and bone alike.

Brandt saw it happening. Saw the impending death of Torres and their ensuing death or capture playing out right in front of her.

Then she saw Specter move.

It wasn't so much a single movement but a flurry of movements in one as he did several things simultaneously. His right hand took the rifle, flipping it up and over to mag-lock it to his back as his left hand snatched up the pistol from that thigh. His right leg propelled him forward, armored boot sole extended ahead of his to connect with the back of the nearest soldier. As his victim flew forward, back arched in a way unnatural for a human body to be able to survive, Specter landed among the five standing figures with his right hand now bearing the other pistol.

Before their heads could even begin to turn toward him, Specter put bullets into the helmets of each of them, working outward from the one holding the big machine gun and ending with those closest to him. They dropped as one, their deaths as close to synchronized as the naked eye was capable of seeing. All of this happened before Brandt could switch her aim.

Specter bent down, grabbed the upper arm of Torres's armor and hauled him to his feet without bending or using his legs like a fully human person would naturally do. He spun him and marched him fast toward the airlock.

"Mech!" Brandt shouted. A big battle mech stepped into view. Specter didn't hesitate, just shoved Torres ahead of him and puffed his chest out just as the booming sounds of 12mm cannons filled the air. The projectiles rocked him, his torso flashing a light blue as they were deflected from hitting his armor.

He whipped the rifle off his shoulder and returned fire, placing a single charged round through the armored spot precisely where the pilot's head would have been.

The mech stopped and appeared to slump and power down. It looked as though the person driving it had just got tired and given up, as opposed to dying horribly inside an alloy coffin.

The soldiers piled inside the airlock, not having the time to take in what they'd just seen. The circular door was already rolling shut behind them to seal it. The firing behind them stopped. Whoever was commanding those troops recognized the dangers of pouring munitions into an open airlock and obviously didn't much care for being vented into space.

Armored soldiers ran toward them, impotently pointing their weapons at them until ordered back by a commander, who stood close enough to glare at them. That mirrored visor stared back at them as they made their escape.

"Everyone sealed? No environmental warnings?" Torres asked. They took a moment to check and none of them had. "Let's do it, then," he said.

Their suits could hold atmosphere in the void, but not indefinitely. The software would react to the change in temperature and pressure, but it took a huge toll on their available battery power to maintain. Given that the suits could sustain them in space for maybe thirty minutes if they just floated and stayed still, the fact they had to run three miles made getting back at all a gamble. That gamble had seemed worth it when confronted with a running battle and no ammunition down a longer, confined tunnel, but now that they faced it Brandt wasn't so sure.

"Bear one-three-four degrees," Specter said, "for a distance of three-point-one-two miles."

"Five clicks?" Eze asked, her hand hovering over the manual emergency release lever for the outer door. "No problem." She dropped the handle.

The air rushed past them, sucked out in an instant. Their suits registered the extreme drop in temperature as they were exposed to the vacuum of space. Eze used a spent magazine to wedge the outer door so that the airlock couldn't be cycled after they left it. They set off, and their slower, more sluggish movements were oddly in contrast to what they had just witnessed.

They moved as fast as they could in the low gravity, running in their powered armor as they would on Earth with long, bounding leaps. On Earth, though, the leaps were much higher and longer in the relative gravity. Soon they were specks, sailing and dropping high over the terrain below as they moved along their projected course.

"Any sign of pursuit?" Torres asked.

"None," came Eze's reply.

"They are moving through the train tunnel now," Specter said worryingly, "monitoring closed-circuit footage. They are leading with battle mech units to utilize heavy caliber weapons."

If it were possible for words to make them move any faster, those would have had the desired effect.

"Halfway," Eze said. "How far behind will they be?"

"Hard to say," Specter said. "Minutes at best."

They reached the approach to the research lab and Torres called them up on the comm channel.

"Base, Torres," he said, his words coming as gasps in between huge leaps of effort. "We're coming in via the surface. Drop the shield to the secondary arrivals bay."

"Understood," came a disembodied voice back to them. "Shield dropping... *now*."

They arrived at the edge of the sunken port—it had been adapted from an impact crater. They dropped down, their movement through the vacuum slow, but their landings still hard enough to jar their bones inside their suits. They ran inside, hitting manual release levers to walk through a smaller airlock.

Inside, the base was still a thronging hive of activity as people poured onto the ship. They ran into the main hangar. Brandt got to see just how big the *Ichi* was up close, as a noise crackled over their comm.

"We got company," a voice said. "Lots of it and they brought big toys along with them."

"The shield will hold," Torres answered. "Everyone onboard now."

The four who had just run over the Moon's uneven, rocky surface took up kneeling positions around the cargo ramp where everyone was boarding. Even those who weren't supposed to be going found themselves swept up. The other factions of the UN would not hesitate to interrogate them to the fullest of their abilities. This caused some upset, and a couple of unwilling scientists were being half-carried aboard and shouting about it.

"We're good to go," a familiar voice said behind them.

Brandt turned to see Paterson, weapon in hand but still wearing his lab coat, gesturing them up the ramp as the smaller steps were disappearing inside the fuselage.

"Have we got everybody?" Torres asked him.

"Everybody except the two CP teams."

"Are they in transit?"

"One is," Paterson said, "but they're an hour away at least."

"Can we pick them up?" Paterson's brow furrowed before he answered.

"We could, but the pilots aren't listed to come along. I don't think we have the luxury of time for a vacuum crossing." Torres paused, no doubt frowning inside his helmet.

"No time," he said. "We'll just have to make do with what we have." His visor flickered toward the three exceptional soldiers he had just fought alongside, reminding himself that Santana, or at least the person with some of his memories, had just saved his ass from dying for the second time.

CHAPTER 20

Onboard the Bōken-Sha Ichi

"Bridge, this is Torres. You ready to get us the hell out of here?"

"Roger, Commander," came the smooth voice of the pilot. "Standing by on your mark."

"Go," he said, steadying himself as a second later the whole ship juddered and vibrated. The engines had been lit and were spinning, and now the pilot ramped up the cycles.

The *Ichi* lifted off. As it rose, all landing skids retracted to provide an unblemished underside, with the exception of two bulbous shapes protruding out with four triangular-shaped minigun barrels sticking out. From the outside a pale electric-blue line lowered over the craft and passed through the shield, which was set to exactly the same harmonic resonance as their own. The *Ichi* carried on rising vertically, turned on one axis to face a direction out into open space, and accelerated away in eerie silence.

"Commander," came the same voice from the bridge. "We have incoming bearing one-seven-eight degrees. They're heading right up our ass, sir."

"Can they catch us?" Torres asked as he strode along the busy walkways inside the ship. It was filled with people all trying to find where they needed to be and carrying armfuls of things they hadn't already packed.

"Calculating… Sir, it depends on how committed they are. It will take them a little over two days unless we go over our top speed."

Torres turned toward Paterson expectantly, Then his face registered annoyance after a few seconds of the scientist not responding.

"What?"

"You didn't hear that?"

"I don't have an earpiece in," Paterson explained lamely.

"Their ships are after us," he explained quickly. "They'll catch us in two days. Can we go any faster?"

"We haven't tested the Fold Drive on a manned flight yet," he said, his eyes wide with horror. "We can't be sure it will work."

"What wouldn't work?" Specter asked.

Paterson stuttered his reply. "We don't know if everyone inside will get turned to mush for starters. And, uh … and…"

"The test you did with the hamster?" Brandt asked. "That worked when it was shielded, right?"

"Well… yes, but…"

"And the unmanned flight tests of the Fold Drive went to plan?"

"Err, yeah…"

"So you have nearly two days to run all the calculations you want."

Paterson couldn't argue with the logic. They certainly couldn't stay. Even if they managed to evade the pursuing ships before they reached Mars, the messages from the unfriendly forces on the lunar base would reach the red planet almost immediately after they arrived. The only option was to take the risk and use the new technology at their disposal.

As they walked toward the bridge, Brandt got Torres's attention.

"I'm down to ten percent," she said, guessing that they all must be close to dead batteries in their suits too.

Torres gestured them to follow him, leading them toward the bridge but veering off to the right before they got there. Empty charging pods were arrayed along one wall opposite another well-stocked armory filled with the new weapons. A man came forward to take their guns and stepped back as they docked their suits and hit the icon for release. The armor split open, revealing starfish forms so they could step out and stretch their limbs. Despite being fitted for them, everyone always felt claustrophobic after a while inside one of them. Torres took a new pistol from the rack and checked it as the others followed suit, with the exception of Specter. He hadn't ditched his armor there. It was a prototype and Hyper wouldn't want anyone poking around at it.

Brandt and Eze followed Torres to the bridge after Specter gave his excuses and left. The two women gave Torres a questioning look, but he dismissed it by saying that Hyper had their own lab onboard the ship and that the robotic man they used to know didn't exactly answer to him.

That reminds me, she thought. *What the hell did he do back there? Did he have a mobile cover device I couldn't see?*

"We need to get to our base on Mars before whatever communication from the lunar surface gets there," Torres explained. "For that we need to arrive ahead of our maximum speed." They all knew that their ships could only travel as fast as their communications. Given their huge leap in propulsion technology, Paterson's Fold Drive was their only hope of achieving that.

"But we have a bigger problem before that," he went on, "because we'll be having company soon and they won't be politely asking us to slow down."

"Surely they will try to capture us if they want the tech?" Eze asked.

"Would you?" Brandt countered. "We're terrorists as far as they know, so why wouldn't they just blow us out of the sky?"

Eze bit the inside of her cheek as she thought about it and accepted the facts. They followed, stepping through the halls of the sleek ship. Their eyes bulged at the new revelations they were faced with. They reached the bridge. Torres scanned his UNID implant by the door as it opened to show the bridge laid out ahead of them.

"Some bureaucracy first, I'm afraid," Torres said as he stood by a commander's large chair.

"We're effectively at sea now," he explained. "So, of the ranking officers, one has to take command as captain." He looked her right in the eyes and waited for a response.

She shifted and cleared her throat. "A few hours ago," she said slowly, "I didn't even know this technology existed. I'm not qualified to take command... Sir."

Torres relaxed visibly, pleased that there was to be no measuring of worthiness based on seniority or personality. Little did he know that her acceptance of his command was based on her respect for how the young wheel had become a man she would gladly follow in battle and beyond.

"Okay," he said. "Thank you. Now, the *Ichi* is nine decks and is a little over two hundred meters from bow to stern. We have the absolute best shields in the known galaxy but seeing as we can't be the only ones developing new tech in secret, we have to expect trouble at some point. We have armaments in the form of four quad twelve-millimeter guns: two fore and two aft."

"How do they fire through the shields?" Brandt asked, unable to stem her excitement at all the new facts she had to assimilate quickly.

"The same way as we pass through the docking shields with our ships," Torres answered. "The charge on those guns is powered by the same singularity reactor that runs the shields, so they have the same resonating harmonics. They pass through, but nothing comes back up the other way, if you follow me."

She nodded.

"Crew quarters are on deck one," he went on, "with bridge, infirmary, armory and other things. Mess hall and crash deck on deck two but no separate messes for officers and enlisted; we're a crew now. Labs are on decks three and four, with the remaining decks being assigned to storage, docking bay and some other non-essentials like a brig."

"How long is she designed to be at sea for?" Eze asked.

"As long as our food supplies last," he said. "Given that we have minimal fresh and vacuum-sealed ingredients onboard, that is as long as our field rations last."

Brandt and Eze both deflated a little, not looking forward to the prospect of living indefinitely on the three daily tablets that provided providing the nutrients their bodies needed. It was a way to survive and stay healthy, but there was no enjoyment to be had in eating in tablet form.

"We have as much as we can carry," Captain Torres said, "and that gives us years if we're forced into it. All the water is recycled, so that will never be an issue either."

"And what exactly is our mission?" Brandt asked.

Torres hesitated, then led the way to an anteroom off the deck of the bridge. "On me."

They walked into a small room with a table and chairs set out. A large screen occupied the main wall and no portholes showed, as with everywhere else on the ship. He tapped at his wrist comm and got Paterson on loudspeaker.

"Are we good to go for sub-space comms?" he asked. "Good to go," Paterson answered. Torres clicked off the link without responding and keyed in more on his device. The main screen came online with a waiting icon as he explained.

"We have another array which is like the Fold Drive at the nose cone. This one fires, for want of a better word, a directed beam, which is very thin and can connect two points in space to allow for instant communication over long distances that would otherwise take weeks."

That impressed Brandt. Ordinarily any conventional message would take a month to reach Mars. The first call went through and a man she didn't recognize answered. Torres filled him in briefly, explaining the situation on Earth and the Moon, that they had been compromised and declared terrorists by at least two territories.

"Go into lockdown," he said. "We have almost two days until we are forced to use the Fold Drive to get to you ahead of our pursuers, but you can bet your ass they've sent word and they'll try to shut you down. Be ready. We'll be in touch."

He killed that screen also and tapped away to bring up another. The loading icon took long seconds to be replaced by a man in an admiral's uniform, looking stressed.

"Torres!" he snapped. "The *hell* have your people been doing? The president is trying to stop all-out war breaking loose down here."

"Admiral," he said. "I believe that the Eastern and African territories are being manipulated by someone into trying to capture or kill us. We were comprom—"

"I know that," the admiral said harshly, cutting him off. "We've surmised as much ourselves and also have the proof that a number of terror attacks by these so-called Choosers are in fact territory-funded and controlled. It's not dissident factions that want us to stay

195

inside our own solar system but other territories. Whether they just want it for themselves first is unclear as yet, but I suspect they just wanted to be the first to have the ability to survey beyond our system."

"Sir," Brandt said. "What about the European territory?" The man shifted uncomfortably.

"They're still on the fence," he admitted. "We're giving them full disclosure in the hope that they ally with us and prevent a goddamned invasion by the East. But it gets worse…"

"Worse?" Torres asked.

"Parts of the other territories want no part of what their leaders are doing, and the Australians are threatening to break away and become a neutral party. As are the Russians."

Jesus, Brandt thought, as she recalled the numbers of the death toll the last time the Earth wasn't unified.

"Our mission, sir?" Torres asked.

"Hasn't changed, son," the admiral answered. "Leave this mess to us, just don't get caught, and bring back proof of life, understood?"

"Understood, sir. Torres out."

The screen went black and he turned to face the others.

"Get settled in," he told them. "Check the manifest for crew allocations. You two are all the CP we have. The team I brought with me were still processing their detainees when it all went south, so I need you to take command of our defense personnel and Hyper security forces. They may not like it, but that's just tough. Make it work… get a grip of them."

Brandt smirked despite herself and the gravity of their situation as he reminded her of the reason she was there.

Taking the steep ladders, they went up to deck one with Eze leading the way. She had already been onboard. Brandt followed, taking it all in and trying to hold in her questions. She had so many that to ask any now would constitute an outpouring of non-chronological nonsense.

"Two-Alpha," Eze said, reading the crew quarters designation from her comm unit's display. "Here." She scanned her arm over the door. It hissed, opening to one side and to reveal a surprisingly well-appointed room, complete with two generous lockers with drawers and a mirror. There was a bathroom comparable to an expensive hotel room and two beds. Though only singles, they were just as generously proportioned.

"Nice," Brandt said, meaning it. She had lived in far worse barracks than that, even as a commander. She had paid for worse hotel rooms than that, come to think about it.

She had no gear to dump, and her sticky civilian clothing clinging to her skin reminded her that she now wore literally everything she owned. As if reading her mind, Eze spoke up.

"You can borrow some of my clothes if you need," she said, earning a smile of thanks from the older woman. "We will also get ship uniform from the stores on deck four."

"Later," Brandt said. "I want to get back to the bridge."

"You can find your own way there?" Eze asked. "I want to check on our equipment."

Brandt walked in, seeing the back of Torres's left shoulder as he lounged to one side in the captain's chair. He craned around to see who had entered the bridge, cracking a smile at the woman in civilian clothing with her disheveled hair.

"Take a seat, Commander," he said, gesturing with his right hand to a similar chair beside him. A man vacated the seat without question and Torres introduced him.

"Brandt, this is my flight officer, Sarvanto," he said. A young man, slim but athletic, smiled at her. "He runs things up here when I'm not around. You'll need to get some stick-time up here to be able to take command shifts."

Brandt shook his hand and felt her warm, strong grip returned as his eyes met hers.

"Pleasure, Commander," he said in an accent that made her blink.

"Swedish?" she asked.

"Close enough. I am from Finland originally," he answered. Sarvanto nodded a slight bow and left them as Torres gestured for her to take the seat once more.

"Thank you, Captain," she responded with the same sarcastic formality he had used when addressing her by her newly restored rank. Before her ass could reach the seat, the door hissed open to admit a man who stormed toward the ship's captain.

"Torres," he barked, "the *hell* are you doing?"

"Levenstein," Torres responded in a cold, almost bored tone. "How can I help?"

"Help?" he said, eyes wide with incredulity and horror. "*Help?* You can help by turning this ship around, immediately, and surrendering it to its rightful owners."

Torres said nothing, but stared at the man who stood directly in front of him and braced his hands on his hips. The posture of defiance was so ridiculous that Brandt let out an unprofessional but involuntary scoff of laughter.

"Lieutenant Commander Brandt, I presume?"

"That's me," she said warily, utterly refusing to add a 'sir' even though the man clearly believed he owned the place. Levenstein said nothing, just scowled at her with a withering look that cried out, 'I'll deal with you later'. He turned back to Torres.

"This ship belongs to the Hudson-Yu Corporation," he said, "as do its contents and certain... *indentured* employees. I order you to turn us abo..."

Torres stood, uncoiling fast to demonstrate the six-inch height difference between the two men.

"Let's make one thing absolutely clear, Levenstein," Torres told him. "*You* don't give *me* orders, you got that?"

Levenstein swallowed, not breaking the eye contact but refusing to back down.

"You are here as a courtesy," Torres went on, "because if you weren't here then you would be in the custody of a hostile territory on the surface of the Moon right now. You will be disembarking when we reach Mars. This ship is under my command, and because we are now on-mission, it is a military vessel and no longer under the control of your purse strings. I therefore invite you to get *the fuck* off my bridge."

Levenstein quailed slightly under the unexpected onslaught of the man he had never seen bare his teeth, but he didn't move.

"Mainframe," Torres said out of the side of his mouth without breaking eye contact, "restrict the access of Levenstein, Ryan, to civilian areas, Hyper laboratory and crew quarters only. Acknowledge."

"Access levels updated," came a robotic reply from the speakers.

Levenstein shot looks at both of them as he stepped back, straightened his coat lapels and tried to walk away with a shred of dignity.

"Who—*what*—was that?" Brandt asked.

"That was Ryan Levenstein," he told her, investing each syllable of the man's name with scorn. "He's a goddamned accountant, but someone at Hyper gave him a brief with the word 'oversight' in it and since then he's been laboring under some misapprehension that he's in charge of anything other than his own zipper."

Brandt chuckled. "Welcome to the private sector."

"Let's just say Hyper can afford the losses. If we're successful, they stand to gain a hell of a lot more. Take a seat."

"Our mission?" Brandt asked lightly.

"It was supposed to be to load up and leave for Mars quietly, offload and pick up some personnel there—more CP soldiers, thank God—and head for our new destination to test the Fold Drive." He sighed in resignation before continuing. "Looks like we'll be forced to test it a little sooner than we expected..."

"And if we can't make it work yet?" she asked.

"Then we have to shoot it out in deep space and shoot it out again when we get to Mars. That, of course, assumes we still have a base there and they aren't overrun in the four weeks it'll take us to get there under normal speed."

Brandt thought about it for a minute before asking the question at the forefront of her mind.

"What idiot-level of imagination calls their mainframe, *mainframe*?"

Torres smiled. "No idea. What would you suggest we call it? Give it a nice girl's name and a sweet voice so men do what it says? Make it a sarcastic asshole?"

Brandt shrugged. "I just think someone could've come up with a better name than that, all I'm saying."

CHAPTER 21

Onboard the Bōken-Sha Ichi

12 Hours Later

Brandt had taken the ladders down to deck three, where she found herself regulation underwear and a fitted flight suit bearing the name of their ship on the left breast. She climbed back up to her quarters and took a shower before she swigged water from a bottle and swallowed down a ration pill to fill her stomach. She slept for almost five hours before waking to the alarm she had set as a backup. She hadn't actually expected to be able to find sleep but had succumbed to exhaustion brought on by adrenaline far more quickly than she imagined possible.

She fixed her hair and face with as minimal effort as possible before stepping into the clean clothes and lacing up the boots she had been wearing with her civilian clothing. She had no waistband to tuck the pistol into, so she swung by the armory on the deck below her on her way to the bridge.

Opening her mouth to ask the soldier for the equipment she needed, he preempted her request and pulled a belt down from a shelf behind him. She smiled her thanks at him, mostly grateful that she wasn't forced to speak before she had found coffee. She strapped the kit around her waist to settle the holster on her thigh before adjusting it to suit. Slipping the gun into the holster, it locked in place and wouldn't release unless her hand was around the grip, just as it did when locking magnetically to her armor. She opened her mouth again to ask for something but stopped as two fresh mags hit the armorer's desk.

"You're the man," she said. "What's your name?"

"Bauer," he said in an unexpectedly German accent. "Heinrich Bauer."

"Brandt," she said, offering her hand to the man. He leaned over the desk to shake it, a slight mechanical whirr sounding as he moved. Her eyes flickered toward the source of the sound and he moved one leg out from behind the desk to show her.

"Lost it in the shootings in Bruges a few years back," he explained.

Brandt nodded. She had been on the other side of the world running some backwater gig as befitted a 'Track' when news of the mass shootings in Belgium had reached them by way of a global terrorism alert. She knew the fighting had been savage and quick there.

"Thanks, Heinrich," she said. "I'll be seeing you."

She left, feeling clean and awake for the first time in a while. When she took stock of their situation she could barely believe that only a few hours before, she had been running a small prison unit and going about the day-to-day before everything flipped upside down.

She walked toward the door to the bridge but before she swiped her implant to open it, the door hissed open and Torres, also clean and shaven and wearing a flight suit like her own, walked toward her with Eze at his shoulder.

"About turn," he called to her. "Deck four." She made a comedic, exaggerated about-face, mimicking the parade ground from when her captain had been just a kid who didn't need to shave, and she had been naively proud of the two white stripes over her shoulder.

They arrived on deck four and swiped their arms over the reader panel where a double door hissed apart to allow them entry to the main lab.

It wasn't quite the grand reveal they were hoping for; sparks flew from a jury-rigged device snaking cables too close for comfort. Torres turned and covered his eyes. Brandt leapt backward and Eze felt foolish as she slowly removed her hand from the handle of the gun she had gripped.

"No, no, no!" yelled Paterson's voice. "Shut it down!"

The sound of something powering down whined through the lab and Paterson emerged in a cloud of something with a datapad held in both hands, as if he were about to brain one of the lab techs. He saw the visitors and almost dropped the pad like he'd been caught playing with matches in a hay barn.

"Hi," he said weakly.

"I was going to ask how things were going…" Torres said, leaving the silence to be filled with answers.

"Fine, fine," Paterson said, just as weakly as before.

"Cut the shit, Jamie," Brandt complained. "Can you do it or not?"

"Do what?" he asked innocently.

"Can you make the Fold Drive work and get us to Mars before our people there are all dead or in custody and we get blasted out of space by the two warships chasing us?" Torres's calm tone quietly betrayed the seriousness of his words.

"Oh, err, not sure. In theory, yes, but if we try it and it doesn't work then we'll never know about it. That's the upside anyway."

"So, if we try it and it doesn't work, then what?" Brandt asked. "We all die?"

"No, we get vaporized and deconstructed at a cellular level and scattered across a couple of light years of open space," he answered, doing nothing to allay their concerns.

"So what's the issue?" Torres asked, to break the very awkward silence.

"Human trials," Paterson answered. "We know it works with organic material because Amelia Earhart over there hasn't turned inside out yet."

"Just need a volunteer to get zapped through and we will know for sure if the magnetic field frequency is right. I'll need us to be at full stop to be certain."

"You got the part where we were being pursued by two ships that will probably launch tactical singularity nukes at us the second they are in range, right?" Torres asked.

"Did you get the part where the test goes wrong and I transport someone out into open space when we're travelling at twenty clicks a second?"

They held each other's gaze for a moment.

"Valid point," Torres answered. "If the test works, how long until we can travel at FTL speed?"

"Three, maybe four hours?"

"Thirty minutes?"

"Three hours tops," Paterson said with what he hoped sounded like finality.

"You'll have an hour," Torres told him, seeing the scientist shrug as though he'd tried his best.

"Fine. I'll just need to fine-tune the last of the emitters for extended projection. In case you haven't noticed, this boat's a little bigger than a person."

"What person?" Brandt asked. "Who is your volunteer?"

"I don't have one yet," he answered.

"You just need someone in a suit to get zapped from one side of the lab to the other, right?"

"Yeah," Paterson said, drawing out the word. "Not quite so simple, but yeah…"

"I'll do it," said a voice from the fringes of the room. It had that telltale metallic twang that could barely be heard.

"You sure about that?" Torres asked him. "Your bosses wouldn't be happy with you taking risks like that…"

"Captain," Specter said as he emerged from the shadows silently to demonstrate his name so aptly. "I am not property, not entirely anyway," he joked, "and I signed no contract to stay out of trouble. Besides, I rather think we are beyond the known realms of risk, aren't we?"

He was still Jake in so many ways, but something about how he spoke, made Brandt believe that he really was a different man. "Doctor," Specter asked, "how long do you need to set up the tests?"

"Two hours tops," he replied. Specter shot an amused glance at Torres at his familiar claim of timeframe.

"Wait," Brandt said in confusion, "I thought you were setting up the tests now. What's all the smoke about?"

"That's steam," Paterson responded with annoyance. "We left the lab in such a hurry that nobody brought the coffee machine. You expect me to work without cappuccino?"

˷

Somehow Ryan Levenstein had got wind of the plan and called up Torres on the comm to formally complain about UNID seizing control of Hyper assets.

"He isn't a toaster, Levenstein," Torres told him. "He's a conscious human being with the freedom and capacity to volunteer, just as he's done. Torres out."

The comm blinked again in seconds and Torres considered having the mainframe cut the man's comm privileges. He decided against that. It was just mean. He wasn't permitted access to the subspace communication array so any message he could send would take nearly a day to reach anyone as it was.

When that avenue didn't work, Levenstein stormed into the lab to order Specter not to conduct the experiment. That avenue became a dead-end even faster. The company cyborg refused his orders and walked past him like he didn't matter.

"Stop," Levenstein said in his most commanding voice. "Power down. Shut down. Power off. Halt. Pause."

Specter rounded on him with inhuman speed and stopped unnervingly still in Levenstein's personal space.

"I am a person with biomechanical implants and prosthesis," he said quietly. "I'm a cyborg, if you feel the need to classify me, but one thing I am *not* is a robot you can give orders to."

He said nothing more, simply turned and walked away. He crossed the room to where Paterson was calibrating a tiny version of the main electromagnetic projector array that stuck out ahead of their ship.

"Good to go, Doctor?" he asked.

"Sure thing," Paterson answered. "Give me a minute." He made a noise of satisfaction, as if he had just won a personal duel with whatever component had been resisting him. He gestured where

Specter should stand, on a wide pad that had the hallmarks of a mobile shield array. A similar pad sat twenty meters away on the opposite side of the wide room and had lab techs buzzing around it like insects, as though Paterson were their queen.

"I need to know what sensations you feel," he said. "Tell me about any pain, nausea, headaches, dizziness... got it?"

Specter nodded.

"Amelia hasn't been too talkative about her experiences, if you catch my drift."

"First hamster to cross the Atlantic solo?" Specter asked with a lopsided smile as the gesture pulled at the old scars on his face. "Why would she not want to talk about it?"

"Exactly," Paterson agreed, more concerned about the test than jokes. "Not too late to pull out."

"Let's just get this done," he replied stoically.

Paterson stepped back and nodded, backing off the sentimentality and getting back to business.

"Paterson to bridge," he said over the comm. "Ready for test."

"Understood, Doctor," Torres's voice came back. "All ahead stop... on your mark. Tell us the second we can go back to full power."

"Ready? Increase power to the micro array," Paterson called out to a lab tech, who tapped at a screen. The command coincided with the thrum and whine of the apparatus ramping up.

Please work, please work, he repeated inside the safe confidentiality of his own mind.

"We're at power," the assistant said nervously.

Please don't turn inside out or explode or disappear...

"Activating on my mark," Paterson called out confidently. "Three, two, one..."

Please work...

"Mark."

Afterward, when Specter was able to speak and stand unaided, when he didn't feel as though he had been crushed through a tiny fraction of the universe to reappear within spitting distance, he was able to explain how it felt.

"Not... not good," he said, dribbling from one side of his mouth.

"Anything more specific?" Paterson asked with genuine remorse for how the man was feeling.

"Weightless... then too much gravity..." he murmured. "No up or down..."

Paterson turned to the terminal beside him, one of the few fixed terminals in the lab, and ran the fastest basic diagnostic he could over the ship's gravity emitter and found it working perfectly normally.

"Anything else?" he asked the disorientated man who seemed to be trying his hardest not to fall off the floor he was holding on to. Specter shook his head, lips pursed as though he either wanted to speak or else throw up; Paterson couldn't say for sure.

"Give me... a minute," he said in an exhausted mumble, "and put me... put me back in..."

"Why?" Paterson asked, unable to comprehend why anyone would put themselves through that kind of pain and risk. In response Specter struggled to flip onto his back and tapped feebly at the device on the inside of his left forearm. It was like their normal comm units, only more compact and was actually a part of his arm. As Paterson watched, a dialogue screen popped up on his terminal asking if he was willing to accept a file. He hit the screen to say yes and a box filled with code flashed up.

"These are... these are shield harmonics," he said as he deciphered them. Specter tapped at his abdomen weakly.

"Calibrate my shield," he muttered breathlessly, "to the same field frequency as the Fold... Drive..."

Specter passed out, his senses ravaged by the unshielded passage through space-time with little protection. Paterson called a medic and had him lifted onto a table to be monitored as he got to work. The tech dedicated to keeping their cybernetic project functioning pushed to the front and opened a compartment under his diaphragm. It popped and slid open, revealing a singularity energy source and combined shield generator. Paterson had been aware of the developments in shielding technology, but this had the look and feel of a prototype about it.

Oh, my God. They did it? If I can get that right, he told himself, *and he can walk out the other end, then the ship and crew can make it.*

CHAPTER 22

UN HQ, American Territory

The six admirals met in a briefing room with a small army of UNID and UNPF advisors. A man bearing no rank in a suit of anonymous uniform gray stood at the head of the table. He called quietly for order as the heads in the room, both physically and those on the dozen or so screens joining in remotely, looked toward him.

"As we all know," he began, "we're on the verge of disaster. We cannot afford a war against even one of these territories on sheer numbers alone, and that doesn't even factor in the threat of guerilla tactics used on our mainlands. We have no choice but to disavow our operatives, make a public statement that they have stolen research-level technology and kidnapped key personnel."

"So we just abandon them? Then what?" asked an olive-skinned woman whose face filled one of the screens.

"Admiral Torres," the suited man said. "I understand your concern, bu—"

"Do you?" she asked.

Her voice wasn't raised. She didn't snap or snarl at him, but her voice carried with it all the genuine power, all the emotional weight of the question. He had no way out. He knew—they *all* knew—that her son was the one at the helm of the prototype ship they had spent three years developing in secret. Other projects, other cutting-edge research, had gone into it, but it was the ship and the potential its technology held that would really change the fate of the human race.

"I do," he answered as empathically as he could. "Not in the same way that you will feel, obviously, but I stake my life on this mission. We have to hope that they can get this done by themselves and come back with irrefutable proof that what they are searching for, what we know is out there, truly exists."

The room was silent, leaving him to close the conversation.

"As of now we must issue a joint statement via the president to disavow everyone involved. We will have to wait to see what happens when, *if*, they reach Mars. But other than that, we have to show the rest of the world that we are against those involved. That means no contact. It means raiding their homes and seizing their assets. It means we have to be seen to be treating them as what the other territories are saying they are: terrorists."

Some of the screens blinked off as the admirals with nothing to say disconnected from the meeting. The representatives to the president would carry their agreement back to him as, no doubt, these orders originated with the politicians first.

They had to hope, because without hope, without an external goal or problem to fixate on, they all believed that the human race was destined to tear itself apart.

CHAPTER 23

Deep Space Between Earth and Mars

"Doctor, how are we looking?" Torres asked over the comm. He tried to keep the urgency out of his voice so he wouldn't panic anyone listening.

"I need another ten minutes," Paterson replied, sounding almost frantic.

Torres pursed his lips to keep himself from swearing foully. He didn't tell Paterson that they didn't have ten minutes—they didn't even have two—because there was no point in giving him a problem that he couldn't affect. He knew that the man wouldn't be offering an inflated estimate of the time he needed, not at this stage when everything was a stake, so he concentrated on everything that he could affect. He also knew that the two smaller craft chasing them had capitalized on the lead they'd gained from their previous stop and were closing to within weapons range.

"All hands," he said calmly with his finger pressed on the button for the ship-wide comm, "battle stations. All non-essential personnel are confined to quarters."

Have I really just given that order? he asked himself, even though his face showed nothing but a hardened resolve.

"Commander?" he asked Brandt beside him. She was already standing. "Can I trouble you to take one of the forward gun positions?"

Her smile said that he could, and that it was no trouble to her at all. She left the bridge, taking the ladder to the upper deck and turning toward the nose where only one more door stood.

She opened it with her implant and stepped inside as the door sealed again behind her, scanning through a second door that acted as an airlock, should the gun-bubble be compromised structurally. She had taken an hour to familiarize herself with the controls of the guns and she enjoyed the feel of the twin sticks in her hands as the seat gripped her tightly.

She settled down, placing the straps over her shoulders and linking them to the ones resting over her thighs. She placed the headset over her skull and activated the weapon system, feeling it come alive to her touch and respond in a way that no neural link she had ever experienced did. The black expanse ahead of her came to life with different colored icons and readings.

"Gun one, ready," she said.

"Gun two, online," came Eze's voice from the bubble directly below her on the ship's underside.

"Gun three, good to go," from a voice she didn't recognize.

"Gun four, hot to fuckin' trot," came a gruff response. Brandt thought it sounded like Horne, the Hyper private military contractor. She made a mental note to meet with him, to explain that he now worked for her. That fact was irrelevant, unless they could escape the incoming singularity nukes they were expecting at any minute.

"All gunners, this is the captain. On my mark we will come to a stop and angle our vector to allow all of you line of sight. Adjust to one-nine-zero degrees, acknowledge."

Another round of acknowledgments sounded off.

"On my mark. All ahead stop and adjust vector... *do it.*"

Brandt sensed no change in inertia as the blackness enveloping them became stationary.

Immediately the HUD on the bubble's glass came alive with flashing red icons, two of them approaching fast as they had yet to react to the sudden stop of their quarry.

They were prepared. As soon as their quad guns centered on the approaching icons, still far too far away for the naked eye to detect a ship in the inky expanse of deep space, more red icons flashed as they appeared on the display.

"Nukes incoming," came a voice from the bridge as the technical officer registered the launches. "Two per ship. Four incoming. Repeat, four incoming."

Their gun's targeting sensors, all interlinked and corresponding, highlighted the nearest missile to each of them. Each warhead, travelling at almost double the speed of the pursing ships, contained a singularity rigged to implode on impact and create a micro black hole that would consume the ship and crush it with the devastating force of physics. No mere atomic detonation could ever expect to match the sheer destructive capabilities of such weapons, but the terminology stuck.

Brandt didn't hesitate. She squeezed the controls and felt the insane vibration of the four triangular-barreled chain guns rattle their charged 12mm projectiles at the incoming missiles. Because of the distance she had fired her third burst before the first struck, chipping away at the ablative armor that encased the hurtling weapons and forcing the missiles to make tiny course corrections to adapt to the forces imposed on them.

The first one blew, the charged ammunition drilling through the casing and activating the detonation. Just a flash, not even a big one,

but the incredible force released by it blotted out a huge section of her HUD.

The ship that had fired it seemed to be captained by someone unaccustomed to the specific physics of fighting in space. Their forward momentum, not adjusted as an experienced pilot would have done after firing a weapon capable of such destruction, carried them straight into the unimaginable pull of the implosion, sucking them in despite the cut and full reverse thrust of engines at the moment they saw it happening.

A flash and the removal of a red icon from the HUD showed that they were gone, but another round of incoming missiles flashed up to prevent any celebration. Brandt switched the aim of her guns and let rip again, firing longer bursts as she used the targeting projection software to lead the missiles in a non-linear approach. More missiles kept coming as they fired, bright electric blue rounds lancing out from the *Ichi*'s guns into the deep black, like lightning as they witnessed other explosive lightshows with the destruction of each incoming nuke.

"Range two-hundred-eighty thousand and closing," came a voice from the bridge. No more nukes came after the fourth one flashed and imploded.

"All gunners," came Torres' voice, "concentrate fire on the ship."

They did, switching their aim as the doomed vessel plunged toward them through the void. It seemed to flounder and turn desperately to escape the onslaught. Near enough to be visible, the ship appeared to glow blue as a million rounds of ammunition drilled the shield surrounding it.

It came apart, exploding as the components flew off in opposing directions, to spin and tumble into eternity until the minute space dust would disintegrate them in years to come.

"Cease fire," Torres said, sounding almost remorseful for what they had done. "Life signs?"

"Reading four, sir," said the voice of the technical officer again, also sounding deflated.

"Viable?"

"Unable to be sure, Captain."

"Helm, take us in, stay at least ten thousand clicks away from those singularities," Torres ordered. "Gunners remain on station but hold fire unless an immediate threat is clear. Acknowledge." They acknowledged in turn, the excitement of the chase and the brief gunfight evaporating for Brandt as she witnessed the destruction wrought on this empty corner of their solar system.

"Damage teams," Torres called over the comm, "prepare to receive wounded."

They came to a stop two hundred meters from the main part of the wreckage where the life signs were registering. A damage team went across in heavy EVA suits with large pods attached to their backs. Brandt listened as the teams worked, hearing how they sealed compartments to maintain atmosphere to place the injured survivors into the pods to transport them back. When the last one was secured, Torres ordered them to download the ship's log before returning.

"Med team, report to the brig. Patch up those survivors and sedate them. We'll leave them on Mars."

"Sir," Horne's voice came over the comm channel, "why bother? They were sent to kill us after all."

"We *bother*," he snapped back, voice full of authority, "because we aren't terrorists and these people are just soldiers following orders."

Nobody raised any other objections.

By the time the team was back on board the channel came alive, this time the technical officer again.

"I read six more ships on a direct course," he cried out, unable to hide his fear. Just then everyone heard Paterson's voice.

"Fold Drive initiated and calibrated," he said. "Ready to jump."

~

As soon as the ship came to a full stop and the massive fuselage vibrated with the firing of the gun-turrets, Paterson had helped the revived Specter into the nearest pod in his lab. He had calibrated the shield harmonics to the Fold Drive resonance, keyed in the command and stepped back.

"See you on the other s—" he said, watching Specter vanish in a shimmer of bending light. He whipped his head around, looking to see if he would arrive at the other end, whether he would simply vanish, or maybe appear as a red mist suspended inside the field. He didn't. He stood facing directly away from him in the same position he had just been in facing toward him.

We've done it, his brain registered in awe. *It finally works.*

He hesitated only long enough to see that Specter was still standing, still able to move and wasn't dead on the platform, then he turned to program the Fold Drive.

Checking the input commands and then checking them again, he hit the transmit button on the comm to tell the bridge they were ready to be the first humans to achieve faster-than-light travel.

~

Torres caught the eye of his helmsman, his own eyes showing the terrified excitement.

"Input coordinates for Mars," he said, his hand half raised as he pondered the order he was about to give.

No time, he told himself. *Get it done.* "Punch it," he said.

CHAPTER 24

Geostationary Orbit Above Mars Base

"Report," Torres said, releasing the breath he had held for the moment it took them to travel what would have taken a month at full velocity.

"All systems green across the board," the technical officer said.

"Are we…" Torres coughed to try and push away the uncomfortable knot in his gut before it threatened to become nausea. "Are we there?"

In answer, the technical officer simply activated the viewscreen to show the red expanse of Mars occupying the lower right quadrant of the view. Torres's shaking finger hovered over the ship-wide comm button again.

"All hands, this is the captain… we have arrived at Mars."

The time spent at FTL, at faster than light speed, had felt like just a minute. They had been in their artificially created wormhole for ninety seconds and his rough mental calculations meant that they had travelled two hundred and forty hours, ten whole days, for each half minute. A month in a minute and a half. The implications of this were unfathomable. He realized he was silent, wasn't giving any orders like a captain should, so he gave a string of instructions to busy the crew.

"Helm, take us into orbit above our base. Gunners stand down. All decks report in any casualties."

There were none, and as his second-in-command rejoined the bridge crew, his flight officer stood to vacate the chair.

"We did it," Brandt said, placing a hand on the shoulder of the younger man, who could hardly believe it himself.

"We did," he breathed in reply.

"Sir, comm link from the surface. Mars control wants us to squawk ident and transfer mission orders... they also want to know why we didn't appear on their deep orbit satellite grid until we arrived."

"Give them our designation," Torres replied. "Resupply and personnel for UNID research base ahead of schedule." The man turned and relayed the information before turning back.

"Sir, they want to know why we we didn't receive our manifest ahead of schedule."

"Tell them we had a comm malfunction early on and didn't send the orders ahead," he ordered. "Stall them, Seaman."

He turned to Brandt. "I need you to take a team to the surface in the *Tanto*. Get our people out and drop off those prisoners. Get back here without a fight if you can. I can't risk taking the *Ichi* to the surface."

Brandt, unfazed by being asked to jump from one fight to another, just nodded. She hit her wrist comm to create a private channel with the people she wanted.

"Eze, Horne, meet me in the armory a-sap," she said. "Horne, bring two of your team. In and out at the surface in a hurry." They acknowledged her, and she called up Specter on the channel to the lab, unable to find his designation on the ship's roster.

"He ain't going anywhere, Commander," Paterson told her. "He needs monitoring after what I just put him through."

"I need a pilot," she told Torres as she made for the door. Torres looked to his helmsman who stood and accompanied Brandt. They left the bridge, walking toward the armory as they talked.

"What's your name?" she asked the young man.

"Rogers, ma'am."

"You a good pilot, Rogers?" she asked.

"No, ma'am," he said, making her stop and look at him.

He smiled. "I'm the *best*."

Brandt looked at him, seeing the utter belief in his youth and his words.

"Well, alright then, meet us at the docking bay." He left, taking the ladder down, and she walked ahead to the armory, where she stepped inside her fully charged armor and took weapons. Horne arrived with his two men and they stepped inside their own rigs and armed themselves. Eze arrived as they were suiting up and nodded her greeting to the commander. She went to leave but Heinrich coughed for her attention and gestured toward the dark tubes at one end of the room.

"Docking bay?" he asked her.

She followed hesitantly as the others stepped inside and dropped down the few decks to arrive directly at their destination. She steadied herself after the brief period of weightlessness to see the back of their smaller ride, about the same size as one of the transports used inside Earth's atmosphere. Rogers was already there, flight suit and helmet on as the twin engines on each stubby wing glowed a pale blue. Four pods were being loaded up the small cargo ramp on repulser carts ahead of them as her team of five climbed onboard.

"Clear the hangar deck." Rogers's voice came over the comm crisply. "Sealing ramp... launch in five, four, three..."

A heavy clunk reverberated around them as they settled into their seats and activated the individual mag-locks to stick their asses to the bench seats. Inertia took hold of them as the ship dropped rapidly, powering itself directly down out of the *Ichi* before the nose came about and dipped to point them toward the surface.

"*Tanto* to *Ichi*," Rogers said. "Clear of docking bay."

The acknowledgment from the bridge was just as crisp and efficient. Brandt sat back and waited for them to reach the surface. She listened to the comm channel again as Rogers sought permission to dock at their base.

"Be advised," came the voice from the other end, "we have UN security forces demanding access to the base at this time."

"Base, this is Captain Torres of the *Ichi. Do not* permit them access, is that understood?"

"Err, understood, Captain," came the uncertain response.

"Obey all orders of the team I have en-route," Torres instructed. "Prepare all personnel to evacuate and purge immediately."

A pause of stunned hesitation on the other end prompted him to speak again.

"Base, is that understood?"

"Understood, sir. Commencing evac and purge now."

~

Brandt stepped off the ramp and left Horne and his two men to unload the prisoners. All around them was a hive of activity, but not in any ordered way. There were maybe twenty people there, a mixture of suited soldiers and techs, and everywhere screens were showing the progress bars of information being wiped from their servers.

"Who's in charge here," she barked loudly.

"That would be me, Grip," said a familiar voice from behind her. She turned to see armor the same as hers, bearing only a shield emblem and a four-letter word.

Zero.

"What the hell..." she said, extending her gauntleted fist for him to bump. The sound of metal clanging together punctuated their meeting.

"I got approached by UNID after Africa and was on the first transport out here. Arrived just over a week ago."

Brandt had no time to process this; the feeling of being around someone else from her past overwhelmed her. She wanted to ask him if he blamed her for the loss of their entire team, if he thought she had screwed up or whether he knew what else had been in play when it had gone down. They had no time. Before she could say anything, an explosion shook the room and vibrated them, prompting screams from some of the techs.

"We need to move, people, RFN!" Zero yelled. The personnel on the base ran to the *Tanto* to start strapping in.

"Gonna be tight," Horne shouted, seeing how rapidly their ship was filling up.

"We can stand," she replied. "Defensive positions."

They took cover ahead of the door to the hangar facing the main entrance of reinforced alloy doors that linked the base to the rest of the Mars colony.

"That's definitely their answer," Eze called out as a second impact hit the door. "They must be using rockets."

Tense moments passed as the flow of people slowed to none behind them.

"All out," Zero called. "Initiate charge timers."

A countdown started on their HUDs, showing two minutes. The door breached, one side slamming open, irreparably damaged in a shower of metal fragments and stone. One piece of rubble flew horizontally past their heads, decapitating a female tech behind them as she ran for the exit.

Fire erupted ahead of them as Horne dropped a mobile cover device and rose behind it. He brandished the heavy squad gun, which his powered armor made look as light as a feather. The insane noise of the thing firing on full auto tore the air all around them to pieces. The rest of the team added their own guns to the fight.

"Go," Horne roared. One of his team was hit dead center in the visor and dropped like a felled tree. "Dammit!" Horne shouted. "Like the man said, RFN, right fuckin' *now*."

They moved, suppressing fire pouring from the old soldier's squad gun. They ran inside the hangar and dropped the door, which they knew wouldn't hold up for long. Two more counters popped up on their HUDs, minimizing after they flashed up on the center of their displays. It was the detonation protocols for the mobile shield array and the suit of the dead Hyper soldier.

They ran for the rear ramp, with the *Tanto* already hovering three feet from the deck. They jumped, sailing through the air thanks to their powerful suit servos, and spilled inside, prompting more shouts of alarm and screams as two more dull thuds of explosions sounded from beyond the door.

"Go!" shouted Brandt, feeling her body pinned to the deck of the small ship as it shot upwards through the shield of the hangar bay.

"*Tanto* to *Ichi*," Rogers called over the comm, "we're on the way, ETA fou— *oh, shit!*" The ship lurched again as the sound of thrumming filled their ears. "*Ichi*, I have incoming. Read two ships, both weapons-hot, copy?"

"Copy, *Tanto*. Standby."

They couldn't hear what happened next as they were out of the thin atmosphere and into the void. The *Ichi* had come about and drilled two long lines of charged fire into the path of the intercepting ships.

One blew apart spectacularly while the other nose-dived back toward the surface, seemingly out of control.

"Thanks," Rogers called out. "Coming in hot."

"Acknowledged," Torres's calm, authoritative voice responded. "All hands prepare to jump when they are back on board."

"Is everyone okay?" Zero said over his suit's loudspeakers. "Is anyone injured?"

Meek shakes of heads replied, and the ship's interior was veiled in stunned silence.

"In about three and a half weeks," Brandt told her old teammate, "they'll get a message to say that we're terrorists flying stolen prototype tech. It won't be too far from the truth, but this shit goes deeper than you think."

They docked, Rogers calling their arrival the second the docking bay doors sealed closed.

"All hands, stand by for jump on my mark... *go!*"

The same strange sensation took them again, shimmering them out of their current reality and into the space between places and times in a way none of them ever truly thought possible.

CHAPTER 25

Thirteen Light Years from Earth

The space this far away from their solar system held an ominous feeling to it, as if they were somewhere and nowhere at the same time. As if they were truly occupying the vast void like a speck of sand in an ocean.

Their first two jumps had been short, only taking the ship far enough away to be in open water, as Torres called it, and to analyze the data from the last period spent at faster-than-light speed. Specter had fully recovered, excusing himself from the main lab even against Paterson's pointed requests. Nobody gave the shadowy man orders. He had the air about him that he was destined for something bigger than the day-to-day toil of routine chores.

The personnel rescued from the Mars base were accommodated, being assigned crew quarters and roles on the ship as well as drilling their respective jobs when—*if*—called to battle stations.

They were so far beyond the scope of pursuit now that they would all be so much older by the time anyone from Earth caught up, assuming that no other territories had developed their own FTL technology.

It was capitalism, Torres knew, pure profit-margin-driven greed and dominance that dictated how they had gone about developing the technology. His superiors hundreds of trillions of kilometers away would have disavowed them by now.

He knew, too, that they would have claimed that their joint research project with the well-known private corporation had been stolen. He knew that they would eventually refuse to comment on the revelation that the terrorists had access to propulsion technology that exceeded anything in the known universe. The *Ichi* and those onboard were on their own until such time as they could make it back with evidence of another Earth. Another habitable planet inside the goldilocks band of a comparable star system. Another place to colonize and inhabit and strip bare of all natural resources before, generations later, they moved on again to somewhere new, like slow-moving intergalactic locusts.

If they made it back, and if they had the irrefutable proof they had been sent for, would the higher powers in their home world have resolved the potential international crisis? Or would they jump back in to a solar system at war with itself?

All of these questions and more burned at Torres as he faced the data terminal in his small office just off the deck of the bridge. It was intended so that the ship's captain could take communications in private from the rest of the crew, but in this case, he stared at the prompt displayed on screen and considered the consequences.

A redundant protocol embedded in the smart onboard operating system—what Brandt had mocked lightly for simply being called 'mainframe'—had alerted him to a communique when they had first jumped beyond the solar system. He had taken it in the captain's cabin and now realized that the communication was a ruse. The display showed him text explaining that further written orders were available to view. That meant, in his experience, that something shady was in play.

He had experienced it a couple of times as a member of the CP teams back on Earth when they had briefed and trained for a mission, only to find it became something very different when they arrived in theater. Those missions were usually assassinations, high-level threat redactions, valuable target acquisitions or however else they made sanctioned murder sound like a normal activity.

This was the same thing, he guessed, but he had no idea how it could be. Taking a deep breath and steadying himself, he hit the command to continue and the computer asked for his identification to be confirmed. He held his left arm over the terminal to allow the biochip to be read, and long enough for the computer to know that it was still implanted in his living body and not just in a dismembered limb. The screen flashed up a new document. It was laid out as standard orders were, only these had a caveat stamped in bold across the top of the page.

CLASSIFIED
TO BE OPENED BY THE SENIOR OFFICER ON BOARD
AFTER DEPARTING EARTH'S SOLAR SYSTEM

Torres swallowed before opening the rest of the document, his eyes growing wider with each line that he read.

~

"Take a seat," Torres told them in an unnaturally subdued voice.

They sat. Brandt, Paterson, Sarvanto, Eze as Brandt's second-in-command, Harris who was the ship's main design engineer and most unexpectedly, the annoyingly short form of Ryan Levenstein. Behind the bureaucrat, and likely intentional to make him feel uncomfortable, loomed the unnaturally still form of Specter.

He sat, careful and formal as he placed his forearms gently onto the table as though testing its surface for unexpected heat. He took a deep breath and raised his eyes to take in the crew.

"Do any of you know how our singularity energy source technology came into being?" he asked quietly, softly, as though he could hardly believe what he was saying himself.

"Well, yeah," Paterson said in a confused voice. "We all do; it's one of the first things we learned in school."

"I know," Torres said, "and… and I'm having a hard time getting my head around this too, but that actually isn't the truth."

The legend of the man who had changed the world was a story known all over Earth. How a pioneering scientist, a Frenchman named Marcus Lachance, assigned to research on the large hadron collider in Europe, had stumbled on a way to create and sustain such a powerful energy source and harness it. At first, it replaced the need to draw electricity from the grid of the research plant. Soon afterwards, they realized the further potential and within a year all of the world's major cities were powered by a singularity. The applications and design were honed and refined so that now, some five generations later, they were able to create minute versions, and more importantly keep them stable, to provide mobile power like they had never known before.

Years after the initial energy source discovery, when war gripped the planet, singularity-powered shields and revolutionary leaps in synthetic alloys used as armor plating emerged. Development of weapons and armor had slowed in the years following the destruction left by the last war, but the creation of the clean energy source seemed to open the door to the next level of human technological advancement.

Lachance hadn't lived to see what his discovery had become—as he irradiated himself in a laboratory accident not long after he had created the first stable singularity—but his legacy lived on hundreds of years later.

Or so they thought.

"All of our technology," Torres said, "from our weapons and armor to our ships' engines and power source, is reverse engineered." He let that hang in the air and said nothing else, just watched as their faces registered the ramifications of what he had just said. Not surprisingly, the physicist and the engineer found questions first.

"Reversed engineered from *what*?" Paterson asked, his voice louder and drowning out that of Harris.

Torres sighed again, this time in disbelief at what he was about to say.

"In the early twenty-second century, a large unidentified craft crash landed in shallow waters off an uninhabited part of what had been Indonesia before it all went underwater." He recited the information deadpan, almost lifeless in his tone, like the briefing document spoke through him without emotion. He *was* feeling very emotional about it. Only he knew what the rest of the document said, so his fear and trepidation killed any excitement dead inside his chest and threatened to spew out of him if he didn't maintain control.

"The craft was powered by a singularity reactor, and that took years to figure out, apparently, but the hull and the materials inside were all analyzed and replicated, just like their shield emitter was."

"But that was a couple of hundred years ago," Paterson said. "How has it taken us this long to reverse engineer the Fold Drive?"

"Because we didn't," Brandt guessed, connecting the dots and wearing a stony expression of suppressed anger. "We stole the designs, right?"

"*We* didn't, but yeah. Doctor Paterson, the final harmonics frequencies you got from the research facility on Earth, when did you get that?"

"About six weeks ago."

"Commander," Torres asked as he faced her, "when was the terrorist bombing that was staged to give a diversion for a covert operation?"

"Six weeks ago," she answered with quiet hostility.

"Exactly," the captain answered. "We *are* using stolen technology, that much is true, so whatever the hell we were told is going on back on Earth is anyone's guess."

"Why?" Eze asked. "What is the point in the espionage?"

"It's the next space race," Paterson said. "First it was the nuclear bomb, then a satellite, then the Moon, then Mars, then deep space. The next thing is travel outside of our solar system and colonization of another planet. It's greed."

His explanation was too accurate, too cynical not to be true. Governments on Earth lied and murdered to achieve the next level of technology before the others, so that they could exploit a new, unexplored horizon and all the riches it would contain before anyone else could. They could charge what they liked for the designs, could ask any price for passage to a new world; they could extort whatever they wanted for the promise of new materials and minerals and ores, mined from planets and moons hundreds of trillions of kilometers beyond the scope of everyone else. Whoever possessed the power to travel at faster-than-light speed held the keys to the galaxy.

And now we hold those keys, Torres thought. He suddenly felt too young and too inexperienced to bear the burden.

The only person not to look shocked at the revelations, not those about the origins of their technology but about the international subterfuge and espionage, was Levenstein. Torres was confident that the others didn't see the expressions he tried to hide but he certainly had, and he planned a private word with the man from Hyper when he next had opportunity.

"So, what are our orders, Captain?" Brandt asked him. He sat back, folding his arms and then unfolding them so that he didn't appear to lack confidence in his words. He slanted his upper body sideways and placed his right palm on the arm of the chair.

"We plot a course to Proxima Centauri," he said. "The sensor array on the ship was calibrated to a spectrum of light similar to what we expect a smaller red dwarf star to emit. Proxima Centauri b, or *PC* and *PCB* as the reports refer to them, is the first port of call on our pioneer mission to find and connect with extra-terrestrial life. We are to survey the planets and moons, and catalogue samples to be brought back. Any relevant discovery, like alien life, is to be reported on the subspace link. Other than that, we are ghosts. Gone. Forgotten. They'll cover everything up on Earth and smile as they race each other to build something else, which is already happening."

"How so?" Harris, the engineer, asked.

"They are building a colony ship, probably more than one, and they need an advance mission report, so they know what the weather is like and what they should pack."

"So we're the recce party before an invasion of another star system?" Brandt asked.

"If you want to view it like that, then yes," Torres replied before he took hold of the room and gave his orders.

"Mister Sarvanto," he said formally, "plot a course for Proxima Centauri, ready to jump on my mark."

"Sir," Paterson said, a look of restrained panic on his face, "we've never jumped that far in one go. We should make smaller jumps until I'm certain about the calibrations; there's no point in scattering us in a billion pieces out in deep space after we've made it this far."

"I'll be guided by you then, Doctor," Torres said. "But I want a jump plotted and ready to go in thirty minutes. Dismissed."

They rose, but Brandt was asked to stay behind. She did, waiting until the others had filed out and the door hissed closed behind them.

"Captain?"

"Leslie, I need you to have the guns manned and a team suited and ready for when we jump into the system; we have no clue what could be waiting for us."

"Understood," she said. "Kyle?"

The use of his given name cut through to him effectively. Despite their history, she would never open the door like she just had when others could hear them. At work they were captain and commander, but alone they were two low-ranking nobodies who now had an elevated paygrade thrust on them.

Perhaps that's the point, she thought. *We're expendable.*

"Yes?" he said, looking her straight in the eye. He radiated honesty.

"That ship," she said, "that *alien* ship that crashed on Earth all that time ago, what was it doing?"

"I don't know," he answered. "The intelligence docket didn't speculate."

"Hostile?" she asked.

Torres shrugged. This was the precise reason he wanted to be ready to fight and defend themselves if the need arose. She nodded and turned to leave but he spoke again.

"You haven't asked the other question I thought you might have..."

She looked at him, eyebrows raised to ask the question in silence.

"If we've made so many technological leaps in the last few generations, what have *they* done?"

Brandt nodded. "Like dropping me and a team into a twentieth century battle?" she said.

"Something like that," he answered. "But I hope not."

"Sarvanto to Captain Torres," the comm channel said. "Ready to make the first jump on your mark, sir."

Torres smiled, showing a confidence he didn't truly believe, but forced himself to.

"Punch it," he said.

EPILOGUE

Centauri System

An ethereal green glow flickered into life in the darkened room. Soft, red light emanated from a few points in the wide, nearly circular room and cast long shadows against the straight edges, which danced in contrast to the smooth, rounded outer bulkhead.

The green glow materialized into a 3D display with three stars and countless planets and planetoids and moons all pirouetting around each other in their own unique elliptical orbital patterns. On that display, far off to the outer edges on the left, a tiny red dot blinked and flashed. It appeared to be stationary but given the scale of the display, that could just mean that it wasn't travelling at faster-than-light speed.

A clicking, gargling noise sounded softly from one side of the chamber and went unanswered. Before the glowing display, a shadow moved, leaning forward out of the high-backed chair it had been lounging in and stretched forward with a three-fingered hand to lightly touch the green hue. The deft movements of the slender fingers interwove with the light show, making the smallest of the three brighter spheres zoom into greater detail. In the void near to that small, slow-burning star was the flashing blip that had brought the display to life. The slim hand reached forward, gently cupping the flashing dot and using one finger to flick outward and almost shoo away the rest of the display.

The hand turned over, opening up as if carefully releasing a butterfly, and a tiny red representation of a ship hung, hovering in the display.

Another hand came forward from the shadow now, revealing part of a smooth, hairless skull and large, dark eyes as the fingers pulled at the display until the ship grew much larger. Those fingers poked and tapped at different parts of the ship as what looked like hieroglyphics came into view to be read and discarded with another casual wave of the hand.

The owner of those hands made a deeper gurgling, croaking noise that had the inflection of a question at the end and a similar noise responded. Had a human heard the exchange and been unable to decipher the language, the tone of voice and hinted body language of their non-verbal communication would have given strong indications of what they were saying.

The hands moved, squeezing the display back down to a smaller size so that the little red star came back into view and the ship returned to being a flashing speck. Lines appeared from the speck, casting off in two directions, which were the course calculations given the unique gravitational fields in the sector. One of those projected lines passed directly through the nearest object orbiting the star: a tidally locked rock where only half of the planet was capable of sustaining any life. The slender fingers stopped moving, staying very still as the brain commanding their movements considered what to do.

The hands clapped together, making the area disappear, and another gesture of the fingers made a dull green outline of a ship appear. This one was obviously of a design that the creature knew well. No confusion or fascination was evident. It placed two fingers on rectangular bars projected on the display and ran the tips gently upwards to power up the craft.

The hands clapped again, and the creature stood; tall and slender with long limbs, it padded softly across the chamber. It stood with its arms held out wide before croaking a single sound. Two others appeared, shorter and stooping in deference as the hands fitted ornate armor to the limbs. They finished their task and stood back; one held out a large helmet in offering as it bowed. The helmet was snatched from the unresisting grip, and the tall alien walked from the room with a curious gait that appeared to be slow and ponderous but covered at least three paces of a fully grown human to each one of its own. It left the chamber via a circular door that closed behind it silently. The two kneeling figures rose and padded excitedly to the display pedestal where they elbowed and jostled one another to reach it first, confusing the display as they both tried to activate it at once. Eventually, one of them pushed the other aside. It radiated sullen jealousy for a minute before the exhilaration of what was happening took hold once again.

The new ship, unlike anything they had ever seen before, came back up and the smaller fingers turned it around and expanded and contracted it to try and examine every inch of the hull. The four bulbous pods protruding from the otherwise smooth lines puzzled them, and the hieroglyphs that came up when these were examined prompted a panicked round of rattling clicks and croaks.

Whatever it was, *whoever* it was, had no idea what they had just flown into.

END OF BOOK ONE

Remember to sign up for my emailing list at **www. devoncford.com**
Follow me on social media for cover reveals, release information and
general shenanigans:
Facebook: @devoncfordofficial
Instagram: @dcf_actual

Also by Devon C Ford
The *After It Happened* series:
(Also on Audible)
1 – Survival (Performed by R.C Bray)
2 – Humanity (Performed by R.C Bray)
3 – Society (Performed by R.C Bray)
4 – Hope (Performed by R.C Bray)
5 – Sanctuary (Performed by R.C Bray)
6 – Rebellion (Performed by R.C Bray)
7 – Andorra (The Leah Chronicles, performed by Kate Reading)
8 – Piracy (The Leah Chronicles, performed by Kate Reading)
9 – Home (Performed by R.C Bray)

The *New Earth* series:
(Also on Audible Performed by Marc Vietor)
1 – ARC
2 -SWARM (with Chris Harris)

The *Burning Skies* Multi-Author series:
(Also on Audible read by Neil Hellegers)
1 – The Fall
2 – Fallout (by Jacqueline Druga)
3 – Uprising (by Chris Harris)